OXFORD BOOKWORMS LIBRARY

Crime & Mystery

The Dead of Jericho

Stage 5 (1800 headwords)

Series Editor: Jennifer Bassett
Founder Editor: Tricia Hedge
Activities Editors: Jennifer Bassett and Alison Baxter

COLIN DEXTER

The Dead of Jericho

Retold by
Clare West

OXFORD UNIVERSITY PRESS

2000

Oxford University Press

Great Clarendon Street, Oxford OX2 6DP

Oxford New York

Athens Auckland Bangkok Bogotá Buenos Aires Calcutta Cape Town
Chennai Dar es Salaam Delhi Florence Hong Kong Istanbul Karachi
Kuala Lumpur Madrid Melbourne Mexico City Mumbai Nairobi
Paris São Paulo Shanghai Singapore Taipei Tokyo Toronto Warsaw
and associated companies in
Berlin Ibadan

OXFORD and OXFORD ENGLISH
are trade marks of Oxford University Press

ISBN 0 19 4230619

Original edition © Colin Dexter 1981
First published 1981 by Macmillan London Ltd
This simplified edition © Oxford University Press 2000

Second impression 2000

First published in Oxford Bookworms 1991
This second edition published in the Oxford Bookworms Library 2000

Illustrated by Ivan Allen/The Inkshed

Printed in Spain by Unigraf s.l.

CONTENTS

PEOPLE IN THIS STORY

Morse is introduced to Anne

She was not a *very* beautiful woman, he thought. He had been introduced to her when he arrived at Mrs Murdoch's party an hour ago. Since then, they had not spoken to each other, but several times their eyes had met across the room. After his third glass of wine he managed to escape from the circle of people he was talking to, and move towards her.

As he passed, he spoke to Mrs Murdoch, a large, plain, cheerful woman in her late forties, who was directing her guests towards the food on tables at the far end of the room.

'Lovely party!'

'Glad you could come,' she answered. 'You must meet some other people! Do you know —?'

'Don't worry,' he said quickly, 'I'm meeting lots of new people! You're looking well. And the boys? How old are they now?'

'Michael's eighteen. Edward's seventeen,' she answered proudly.

'Really! Doing their exams soon, I suppose?'

'Michael's doing his next month.'

'Confident, is he?'

'I don't think it's good to be too confident, do you?'

'Perhaps you're right,' he said. Had he noticed a worried look in Mrs Murdoch's eyes? 'And Edward?' But she had moved away to talk to her other guests. So he was free to go up to the attractive woman, who was looking at the food.

'Looks good, doesn't it?' he said to her.

'Hungry?' she asked, turning towards him. Now that he was close she looked more attractive than ever, with her wide brown eyes, clear skin and generous mouth.

'A bit,' he answered.

'You probably eat too much,' she said, laughing, and put her hand lightly on his stomach. Things were going well, he thought. But as he watched her slim figure turn and bend over the food, he suddenly felt depressed and hopeless. After all, he was fifty and going bald and she was more than ten years younger. It was time he stopped chasing women.

He decided to sit and eat in peace, and found a place alone at a table. A minute later he was surprised to see her coming towards him.

'Do you mind if I join you?' she asked.

'Not at all,' he answered. 'I just thought you'd prefer to find someone younger to spend the evening with.'

'They're all very boring.' She raised her glass to her lips.

'Well, I'm just the same as all the others,' he replied.

'What do you mean?' she asked. Their eyes met again.

'I find you very attractive, that's all,' he said quietly. She did not answer, and they both went on eating silently.

'You know,' she said, 'when most men say that, it just means they want to have sex.'

'There's nothing wrong with that, is there?'

'Of course not! But that's not the only thing, is it? I mean, you can like a woman for what she *is*, not just what she looks like, can't you?'

'I don't know much about women,' he said sadly. But her hand reached for his under the table, and held it.

2

'I find you very attractive, that's all,' he said quietly.

'Look,' she said, 'let's forget about the other guests. Why don't we just sit here together all evening?'

'Why not indeed!' he said. 'Now, have some more wine, and tell me a bit about yourself.'

She told him she had studied modern languages at university, and then worked as a foreign sales representative for a small publishing company in Croydon, which was managed by two brothers. She had travelled on business (and pleasure!) with one of the brothers. She had stayed in that job for eight years, as the company got bigger and her own salary rose. And then she had left.

'Why?' he asked sharply.

'I'm not sure. I just wanted a change. So I took a job teaching German in a very large school in the East End of London. But I found it so difficult trying to teach children who just weren't interested in school! And the other teachers, well, the men were a bit *too* interested in me! So I left after a year or so. In the end I came back to Oxford, advertised for private students, bought a little house, and here I am!'

She had missed out something, he thought. Hadn't Mrs Murdoch said she was married? And there were other holes in her story. But he said nothing, just sat there drinking and looking at her happily. It was a few minutes after midnight and some of the guests were already leaving.

'What about you?' she asked him.

'I'm not as interesting as you are,' he said. 'I just want to go on sitting here with you.' He was beginning to sound rather drunk, but the woman felt strangely interested in him. They were holding hands again, and talking like old friends.

4

At twenty past one the phone rang, and Mrs Murdoch came to say it was for him. He went to the phone in the hall.

'What? Lewis? What the hell do you have to — ? Oh. Oh, all right. Yes! Yes! I *said* so, didn't I?' He banged down the phone and returned to the woman.

'Anything wrong?' she asked, a little worried.

'Not really, it's just that I've got to leave, I'm afraid —'

'But you've got time to take me home, haven't you? Please!'

'I'm sorry, I can't. You see, I'm on call tonight and —'

'Are you a doctor?'

'I'm a policeman.'

'Oh God!'

'I'm sorry —'

'Don't keep saying you're sorry!' There was a moment of silence, then she said, 'No, *I'm* sorry, for getting cross, I mean. It's just that . . . I wanted . . .' She looked up at him with disappointed eyes. 'Perhaps it's fate . . .'

'Nonsense! There's no such thing!'   ~realist~

'Don't you believe in fate?'

'No! Look, when can we meet again?' he asked urgently. She wrote her address quickly on a piece of paper – 9 Canal Reach – and gave it to him. He took it, and turned to leave. But he had to ask the question he'd been thinking about all evening.

'You're married, aren't you?'

'Yes, but —'

'To one of the brothers in the Croydon company?'

She paused a moment before answering. 'No, I was married long before that. I was silly enough to marry when I

5

was nineteen, but —'

Just then a tall, youngish man entered the room, walked towards them and said, 'Ready, sir?'

'Yes.' He turned and looked at her for the last time, wanting to say something, but unable to find the words.

'You've got my address?' she whispered.

'Yes, but I don't know your name,' he replied.

'Anne. Anne Scott. What's *your* name?' she asked.

'They call me Morse,' said the policeman.

'Where are you taking me to, Lewis?' Morse asked, as the police car drove fast through the streets of Oxford.

'Out of town, sir, Kidlington. A man's stabbed his wife there. He came into the police station and admitted it.'

'It doesn't surprise you, Lewis, does it? In most murder cases there's an obvious person to accuse right from the beginning. Usually he's arrested close to where the murder happened, and in about 50% of cases he and the murdered person knew each other well.'

'Interesting, sir,' said Lewis politely.

'By the way, Lewis,' said Morse, 'where's Canal Reach?'

'It's in Oxford, sir, near the canal, down in Jericho.'

The first death in Jericho

Oxford is one of England's most beautiful cities. The fine old university buildings and churches in the town

6

centre are visited by large numbers of tourists. Unfortunately, many ancient streets of houses have been destroyed to provide modern shops and offices. However, there is a part of Oxford where there are hardly any new buildings, and where people live undisturbed in their old houses as they have always done. This area, in the north-west of the city, between Walton Street and the canal, is called Jericho. Its houses are small and narrow, and were built for factory and railway workers over a hundred years ago. Not many tourists find their way to Jericho.

On Wednesday October 3rd, about six months after Mrs Murdoch's party, Inspector Morse was driving through Oxford. As he turned into Walton Street he suddenly realized he was in Jericho, and immediately thought of Anne Scott. He had not forgotten her, of course not, but an affair with a married woman had seemed rather complicated when he had considered it the morning after the party, so he had not contacted her. But he was thinking of her now . . .

It was his free afternoon and he had a special reason for coming to this part of the city. As a member of the Oxford Book Club he had been invited to a talk on English poetry, to be given that Wednesday evening by a well-known Oxford professor. The Book Club had also arranged a second-hand book sale just before the professor's talk, and asked members to provide books to sell. So Morse was on his way to deliver some of his old books to the Club's address in Walton Street. It was 3.25 p.m.

But something made him decide to turn off Walton Street and drive slowly towards the canal. Surely Canal Reach must be very close? The narrow streets made parking difficult but at last he managed to park in a street next to the canal, and walked back into Canal Street. He thought he saw a parking ticket on a large, light-blue Rolls Royce parked the other side of the street, but parking problems no longer interested him. He had arrived at Canal Reach, and now he hesitated, wondering why he was there, and what, if anything, he had to say to her . . .

It was a short, narrow street of five small houses on each side, closed to traffic by three solid posts at one end, and by the canal at the other. Although it was getting dark, there were no lights at any of the windows. Morse walked down the left side, past numbers 1, 3, 5, and 7. And there he was, standing in front of the last house, number 9, feeling strangely undecided. Where were his cigarettes? He must have left them in the car.

Morse knocked twice, but there was no answer. He was almost glad. He wasn't sure he wanted to see her anyway. But he stepped back and looked at the house. The curtains were closed in the downstairs room. Upstairs – just a minute! There *was* a light, coming from the other bedroom at the back of the house, perhaps? He waited in the heavy rain, but nobody came. He felt depressed. Why had he come? He'd had too much beer at lunch-time. That had made him think of the attractive woman he'd only met once. And then he thought he heard a noise inside the house. He knocked again, very loudly, and pushed the door. It opened.

'Hello? Anyone there?' The front door led straight into the sitting room. Morse looked around, noticing all the details.

'Hello? Anne?'

He knocked again very loudly, and pushed the door.

Hanging at the bottom of the stairs he saw an expensive-looking brown leather jacket, still wet from the rain. But although he listened very carefully, he could hear nothing. Why had she left the door unlocked? But he often forgot to lock doors himself. As he closed the door quietly behind him and stepped onto the wet pavement, he looked up at the house opposite, number 10, and was surprised to see a tiny movement of the curtains at the upstairs window. Was he being watched? Turning back to look at Anne Scott's house, he thought warmly of the woman he would never see again . . .

It took him some time to realize that *the light upstairs had been turned off. There was somebody in Anne's house.*

The professor's excellent talk on English poetry that evening was obviously enjoyed by the Oxford Book Club members. Morse clapped loudly too, and promised himself he would read more poetry and come to more talks like this. Discovering more about language, poetry and music, that's what's really important in life, he thought. He decided to have a drink in the members' bar before going home. Perhaps his friend the chairman would join him.

Sitting there alone with his beer, he heard the siren of a police car or ambulance outside in Walton Street. A traffic accident somewhere, perhaps.

'You look lonely. Do you mind if I join you?' She was a tall, slim, attractive woman in her early thirties.

'Delighted!' said Morse. They talked about the professor, and poetry, and Morse, looking into her large bright eyes, hoped she would not go away.

'You're Inspector Morse, aren't you?' she said, smiling.

'How did you know?' he asked, surprised.

'I'm the chairman's wife,' she laughed.

Married! thought Morse, disappointed. Another siren sounded from Walton Street. The chairman called from the bar, 'I'll bring you another beer, Inspector.' And when he arrived with the drinks he said, 'There's a bit of trouble near the canal. Police cars, ambulance . . . Something's happened.'

But Morse was no longer listening. 'They may need me,' he said, and leaving his second beer untouched, he walked quickly out. His throat was dry and he wanted to run. But somehow he knew that he was already much too late. Perhaps he had always been too late. And as he turned into Canal Street, there, ahead of him, stood an ambulance and two police cars. He explained who he was to the policeman guarding the entrance to Canal Reach, and was allowed to pass.

Inside number 9 the sitting room looked almost the same as he had seen it earlier. This time there was no jacket on the stairs. In the room was a young policeman, Constable Walters.

'Who's investigating this?' Morse asked him.

'Inspector Bell, sir. He's in the kitchen, with the body.'

Morse shook his head weakly and wondered what to do or say. What *could* he do? He couldn't help her any more.

'Do you want to see the body, sir?' asked the constable.

'No-o. No, I just happened to be in Jericho . . . Er . . . How did she die?'

'Hanged herself. Stood on a —'

'How did you hear about it?'

'Phone call from somebody, sir, we don't know who. It's strange, nobody could see into the kitchen from the back of

11

the house, so how did he know —'

'Did she leave a note or a letter?'

'We haven't found one yet.'

'Was . . . er . . . the front door unlocked?'

The policeman looked interested. 'It *was*, sir. We just walked straight in, and anybody else could have done the same.'

'Was the door to the kitchen locked?'

'No, sir.'

'Have you moved anything in here?'

'Nothing, sir, well, nothing except the key.'

Morse looked up quickly. 'Key?'

'Yes, sir. It looked quite new. It was lying on the carpet near the front door. Someone could have pushed it through the letter box.'

Morse turned to go. That afternoon he had noticed a large black umbrella near the door. It was no longer there.

'Have you moved anything, constable?' he asked.

'You've just asked me that, sir.'

'Oh yes,' admitted Morse. 'I was just . . . er . . . thinking, you know.' He opened the front door and hesitated. 'Were there any lights on upstairs?'

'Oh no, sir. Black as night up there.'

Morse thought of the woman who was now stretched out on the cold floor of the kitchen. Dead, dead, dead. A warm, attractive, living, loving woman – why had she hanged herself? Why? Why? Why?

He felt unable to think clearly, even when he was out in the narrow street again. Strange, he said to himself, Walters told me there were no lights on upstairs when they arrived, but I saw . . . Suddenly he noticed a strong smell of fish. It came from a basket attached to an ancient bicycle outside number 10.

He pushed through the little crowd of local people discussing the death, and found the nearest phone box. Inside, the phone book was open at the page for POLICE. This must be the phone box the unknown person had used to report Anne's death. As he bent over the book, he knew he was right. *There was the smell of fish.*

He walked quickly away from Jericho and all the way home to his flat in North Oxford, where he sat miserably without moving for an hour. Then he listened to his favourite piece of Mozart. Sometimes the beautiful music made him forget crime, and death, and sadness. But not tonight.

Suicide or murder?

Inside 9 Canal Reach, Constable Walters entered the kitchen.

'Inspector Morse was here a few minutes ago, sir,' he said to Inspector Bell, a tall, black-haired man.

'What the hell did he want?' asked Bell crossly.

'He just asked a few questions, sir. Do you know him well?'

'I suppose so. We've worked together once or twice. He's a strange man, bloody strange.'

'People say he's clever.'

'Yes, that's right.' Bell was an honest man. 'Cleverest detective I've ever met. Cleverer than most of us anyway.'

'He never married, did he?'

'Too lazy for that. Likes spending his free time in pubs, or listening to Mozart!' Bell laughed. Then he stopped and looked sharply at Walters. 'Now perhaps you'd like to tell me exactly what questions he asked?'

As Walters repeated Morse's questions, Bell listened carefully. Of course it was strange that the front door wasn't locked, and he still didn't know who had rung the police. But he had only just started investigating the case. He would know more details soon. Anyway, details were not really necessary, because it was a simple case of suicide. She had hanged herself by attaching a rope to the ceiling, standing on a chair and kicking it away. As an experienced police officer he had seen many suicides like this. Perhaps when his men searched the house they would find a note explaining why she had killed herself. There was only one thing that worried Bell, and he hadn't told the police doctor or Walters or any of his men about it. How does a woman, at that terrible fatal moment, kick the chair away so that it lands almost two metres away from her? But it didn't really matter, he told himself. He was sure it was suicide.

Bell did not find the suicide note he was looking for. But there *was* at least one note which Anne Scott had written the night before she died – a note which was delivered and received.

From number 10 Canal Reach, George Jackson continued

14

to watch the house opposite. He was sixty-six, short and thin, with watery blue eyes. When he lost his factory job, he had moved here. Although he had no real friends, most people in Jericho knew him, because he was good with his hands and did odd jobs for his neighbours.

He did not often drink much, but that Wednesday evening he stood in his dark front room drinking whisky. He knew he could not be seen, standing right at the back of his room, with no lights on. The two fish he had caught that morning were in the kitchen, but he wasn't hungry. He saw the police arrive, then a doctor, then two more policemen, then a man of about fifty who was going bald. *A man he had seen before, that very afternoon, at about 3.30, entering number 9.* Jackson watched, drinking his whisky, and feeling much less anxious than a few hours earlier. Only one thing worried him – had anyone seen *him* then? Anyway he had invented a clever little lie to protect himself. He finished his bottle of whisky and went on watching until the police finally left.

Earlier that Wednesday evening, in an expensive, well-furnished house in Abingdon, a small town near Oxford, Celia Richards heard her husband's car arrive. He was very late, and dinner had been ready for a long time.

'Hello, darling, sorry I'm late.'

'You could have phoned me to tell me you'd be late.'

'I just said I was sorry, darling, didn't I?' He sat down and put a cigarette in his mouth.

'You're not going to smoke that just before we eat, are you?'

15

George Jackson continued to watch the house opposite.

'Oh, all right.' He put the cigarette back into its packet. 'But there's time for a drink, isn't there? What would you like?'

Celia suddenly felt better, and – yes! – almost glad to see him again. She'd already had two large drinks herself.

'You sit down, Charles, and have that cigarette. I'll get the drinks.' She forced herself to smile at him while handing him his whisky. 'Did you see Conrad today?' she added.

'Conrad?' Charles repeated. He seemed to be thinking of something else.

'Yes, Charles, your brother Conrad. You do work with him, don't you?' she replied sharply.

'Oh, *Conrad!* Sorry, darling. I'm a bit tired, that's all. Conrad's fine, yes. But our meeting finished at lunch-time, and then I had some . . . er . . . rather difficult business to complete.'

Celia was no longer interested. She sat there with her drink, an attractive, rich woman in a cloud of unhappiness. She knew, she was almost sure, that Charles had affairs with other women. Had he been with another woman today? She had so much to worry about. And the worst thing was knowing it was her fault that Charles needed other women. She had never been interested in sex, and somehow they had never seriously considered having children. She would be thirty-eight soon. It was really too late now.

On her way to the kitchen, she saw Charles's large black umbrella near the front door. She put it back where it was always kept, in the Rolls Royce, parked outside the house.

By 8.30 they had finished their dinner. Celia had not spoken at all during the meal. Her head was full of wild

17

thoughts, and the person she was thinking of was her husband's brother, Conrad.

It was at 9.15 that evening that an unknown person rang the police and told them to go to Anne Scott's house in Jericho.

At exactly the same time that Inspector Bell and Constable Walters were discovering Anne's body, Edward Murdoch, the younger of the two Murdoch brothers, was reading in bed, in the house where Morse had first met Anne Scott. The book he was reading was by Kafka, in German. Although Edward was not very good at German, he had shown great interest in the language since starting private lessons with Anne Scott. Now he put the book down, turned the light off, and began to think about her. Had his brother Michael really had sex with her? That's what Michael said, but he didn't always tell the truth, and Edward would never have believed it – until last week. For the hundredth time he remembered those few exciting moments . . .

When he arrived at her house for his lesson last Wednesday afternoon the front door was locked, which was unusual. He had to knock, and she appeared at the door in her night clothes.

'Edward! Come in! I'm sorry, I was asleep!' Her long hair fell to her shoulders, and she was smiling at him. Could it be that she was happy to see him? She held his arm and took him upstairs to the back bedroom, where he always had his lessons.

'I'll be very quick, I promise,' she said, laughing, as she ran into the front bedroom. Edward's mouth felt dry.

18

A few minutes later he heard her call.

'Edward? Edward? Can you come here a minute?'

Her bedroom door was half open, and the boy stood by it, hesitating. He would never forget how she looked. She was standing near a large double bed, and all she was wearing was a grey skirt. He could not take his eyes off her beautiful body.

'Haven't you seen a woman's body before, Edward?' she laughed. 'Be a darling, and help me fasten this skirt.'

He managed to do it, his hands clumsy and trembling.

'Thank you, now go and read some German. I'll be with you soon,' she said. He tried hard to concentrate on Kafka for the rest of the lesson.

That was a week ago. He had been looking forward to his 2.30 lesson with her today, but at about 7.30 this morning a letter had been delivered, by hand, addressed to him. It said:

> Dear Edward,
>
> I'm sorry but I won't be able to see you for our usual lesson today. Go on reading Kafka – you'll discover what a great man he was. Good Luck!
>
> Anne (Scott)

It was disappointing, but in a way it was exciting too. Perhaps next week he could call her Anne? He'd always

19

called her Miss Scott up to now. He did not understand how final it was.

When Morse woke up next morning, Thursday October 4th, he suddenly remembered he had left his car in Jericho.

'Bloody hell!' he said, and rang up Sergeant Lewis, who came to collect him and drive him to Walton Street. There they found Morse's car where he had parked it for the Oxford Book Club talk. Parking problems! thought Morse. It gave him an interesting idea.

Walters investigates

Constable Walters and Inspector Bell searched the two small bedrooms of 9 Canal Reach, looking for clues. They found large piles of letters in the drawers of a desk. Anne had obviously tried to arrange them in some kind of order. They spent some time looking through the letters, but in the end Bell only seemed interested in three things, a recent letter from Anne's mother, an address-book, and a desk diary.

'This should be helpful!' he said, handing the diary to Walters. He pointed to the page for Tuesday October 2nd: 'Summertown Bridge Club 8 p.m.,' and then to the page for the next day, Wednesday October 3rd, the day of Anne's death: 'E.M. 2.30.'

Next day Walters, who had been told to discover as much as possible about Anne's life, returned from his investigations to report to Bell. He was rather pleased with himself for finding so many details about her.

She had studied hard at school, and been intelligent enough to get a place to study modern languages at one of the famous Oxford colleges. Unfortunately she had fallen in love with another student, John Westerby, fallen into bed with him and become pregnant. Her father, a strict man, refused to see her ever again, and died soon afterwards, but Anne and her mother were still in contact. John and Anne were married, and then they left Oxford for a long summer holiday. During that time the young couple must have decided not to have the baby, as there was no sign of a baby when they returned. They separated almost immediately. After that Anne's working life was easy to follow. It was as she had explained to Morse. John Westerby had been killed in a car crash near Oxford about a year ago.

Bell was listening as Walters finished his report, but he was busy and didn't have time to worry about the past life of a woman who had stopped herself ever feeling miserable again. He knew, however, that there would be questions to answer at the inquest. Why had she done it? Was anything worrying her? Bloody stupid questions! Of course something was worrying her! Everybody was worried about something, health, money, sex, family . . . Bell shook his head sadly. The real mystery to him was why so many people *went on* with life, uncomplaining.

'Have you discovered who E.M. is yet?' he asked.

21

'No, sir,' answered Walters, obviously disappointed. Anne used to give several private lessons a week, but she kept no list of names, and the neighbours were not sure they would recognize any of her visitors.

'Forget it, Walters,' said Bell, smiling. 'Perhaps it was the Electricity Man! Let me tell you something. That woman killed herself. I know. I've been finding suicides like that for the last twenty years. So, why did she do it? Well, we'll never be sure. People get unhappy, you know. Don't think that life is wonderful, because it isn't. It's bloody awful. There are crashes and wars and earthquakes and diseases – so don't be surprised if you find one or two people who feel life's too much for them!'

The young constable wondered whether Morse would investigate this case more carefully than Bell. He looked at his boss.

'And if you're worried about it,' continued Bell, noticing the look, '*you* go and find some more information. And find some witnesses for the inquest too, would you?'

So Walters went back to Canal Reach that afternoon. Morse's question about Anne's front door was still worrying him. Next to number 9 was number 7, where a grey-haired old woman lived alone.

'I just wondered if Anne Scott ever left a key with you, Mrs Purvis?' he asked politely when she opened the door to him.

'Yes, er, she did, about a year ago. She never asked me for it, but I expect she thought it'd be useful if she lost hers.'

Was Mrs Purvis hiding something? She didn't seem very confident. Walters took Anne's key away with him. He now

22

had three keys to Anne's front door. The second was the new one which had been discovered inside the front door, probably pushed through the letter box. And the third was the one which Anne herself must have used, and which she'd kept in the sitting room.

The locksmith who had a shop in Walton Street remembered cutting two new keys for Anne Scott nearly two years before.

'How many keys do you get when you buy a house in this area?'

'Two, usually,' answered the locksmith.

'So in the end she had four keys,' said Walters slowly.

'It would be more accurate to say that she had four keys *at one time*, wouldn't it, constable?' replied the locksmith.

Walters was beginning to dislike the man.

'Anything else you should tell me?' he asked sharply.

The locksmith said nothing until Walters was almost out of the door and then – '*Somebody* in Canal Reach knows something about those keys. *Try number 10.*'

Interesting, thought Walters, as he walked back to number 9 and used Mrs Purvis's key to open the door. From the kitchen window he could see that the wall between the back garden and the canal had recently been repaired. He went up to the front bedroom and stepped right in front of the window. He was delighted to see a tiny movement of the curtain at number 10, opposite. So Anne's bedroom *was* being watched!

It was clearly important to visit number 10. He went straight downstairs and across the road to interview George Jackson.

'Did you know Anne Scott well, Mr Jackson?'

'Not really. Nice woman, but I never knew much about her.'

'Did she ever leave her key with you?' Walters wondered if he could see fear in Jackson's cold eyes. The man hesitated.

'Well, yes, she did. I did a few odd jobs for her, you know. So even if she wasn't in, I could go into her house any time.'

'Was it you who repaired her garden wall?'

This time Jackson certainly wasn't afraid, he was proud.

'You saw that?' His small face shone with pleasure. 'A neat little job, wasn't it? I finished on Tuesday afternoon. You can ask Mrs Purvis if you don't believe me. She saw me in Miss Scott's back garden. You ask her!' Jackson looked confident now. Walters felt sure he was telling the truth.

'So you've still got the key?'

'No, I forgot to give it back to Miss Scott when she paid me on Tuesday afternoon. But I remembered on Wednesday, so when I got back from fishing in the morning, I took it over to her house in the afternoon —'

'You did?' Walters felt strangely excited.

'And I just put it through the letter box,' finished Jackson.

'Oh.' So it was all very simple. How disappointing. But there were other questions to answer. 'Was the door unlocked?'

Jackson thought for a moment. 'I don't know,' he said. 'I didn't try to open it.'

'Perhaps, Mr Jackson, you saw someone else going into number 9 sometime in the afternoon?'

'I'm getting old, I don't remember things as well as I used

24

to,' replied Jackson. 'But I think there *was* someone. Yes, he just walked in, and then a few minutes later he walked out.'

'What was he like?' asked Walters eagerly.

'Never seen him before. About fifty, going bald.'

Walters needed time to think about this new clue, but Jackson did not stop. 'But I think I saw him *later*.'

'What!'

'He went in there while all the police were there, after they found the body. You let him in yourself, I seem to remember. So he must be a policeman, mustn't he?'

After Walters had left, Jackson sat in his tiny kitchen, drinking tea and feeling very pleased with himself. He was sure the policeman had believed him. Anyway, he had told the truth, at least about the key. His plan was very successful so far.

Later that day, in his interview with the secretary of the Summertown Bridge Club, Mrs Gwendola Briggs, Walters discovered that Anne had been a member for six months. She hardly ever missed their regular bridge evening on Tuesdays. Last Tuesday she had played with Mrs Raven, old Mr Parkes and young Miss Edgeley, and they had finished late, at 2.45 in the morning.

But unfortunately none of these three had any more information to offer. In bed that night Walters thought hard about the case. It certainly seemed to be suicide, but he had found no reason for it yet. And how had Anne Scott gone home after playing bridge, the night before her death? By taxi? By bicycle? With someone? According to the medical report, she had been dead for about ten hours by the time

25

the police found her. Why was her front door unlocked? Had she forgotten to lock it? Anne had her own key, Mrs Purvis had one, and Jackson . . . Jackson could have unlocked the door with his key, walked in and discovered the body in the kitchen! He could have moved the kitchen chair too. But why hadn't he phoned the police immediately, from number 9? Did he feel guilty? Perhaps he stole something, perhaps there was money lying around in the kitchen. And what about that other mystery, Morse? It must have been Morse who Jackson had seen coming to the house in the afternoon. Why had he come? Was he taking German lessons with Anne? Walters remembered Morse's question that night. 'How did she die?' Surely nobody had told him it was a woman who was dead. So *how did he know that?*

Suddenly Walters jumped out of bed, ran to the phone book and turned the pages rapidly until he came to the Ms. There it was, in black and white. 'Morse, E.' Was *Morse* the 'E.M.' who Anne had been expecting that Wednesday afternoon at 2.30? Perhaps Morse had a key to number 9 too. If he, not Jackson, had walked in and discovered the body in the kitchen, why hadn't he reported it?

Walters found it difficult to sleep that night. It was a serious thing to accuse an experienced police officer of not reporting a crime. But what was worrying Walters was that Inspector Morse could be guilty of something even worse.

~

It was not only Walters who had difficulty in sleeping that night. Charles Richards could not sleep either. He could not stop thinking of the stupid mistake he had made. When his wife Celia saw that long blonde hair on his dark-brown jacket, he should have simply laughed about it. Instead, he invented a long, complicated explanation, which she obviously did not believe. He remembered seeing the anger and jealousy in her face. In the past she may have guessed about his love affairs, but now she *knew* the truth. He felt guilty and depressed. He was growing old, losing his hair, losing his teeth, and now losing his wife too. He was drinking and smoking too much, and having sex too often . . . How he hated himself sometimes!

Still feeling tired, he got up early, and drove to his office in the centre of Abingdon, even though it was Saturday morning. He and his brother Conrad usually spent some time in the office at the weekend, discussing business together. But today Charles told his secretary that he did not want to be disturbed, and, smoking cigarette after cigarette, sat at his desk, feeling sorry for himself and wishing he could change his character. Why didn't he stop smoking? Why didn't he stop having girlfriends? How could he go on hurting his wife Celia like this?

At 10.15 he decided to talk to Conrad. They had always been good friends, and Conrad, younger, kinder and more serious than Charles, had always been very understanding about his brother's many affairs. Charles rang Conrad at home.

'Not coming to work today, Conrad?'

'I'm just off on that business trip you arranged, remember?'

'Oh, I'd forgotten. Look, Conrad, can you . . . er . . . help me?'

'Again?'

'This is the last time, I promise. You see, I'd . . . I'd like an alibi for yesterday afternoon.'

'That's the second time this week!' Conrad sounded unusually cross.

'I know, but I promise it won't happen again.'

'All right. What do you want me to say if Celia asks?'

'Say we were in London all afternoon on business. I . . . we . . . er . . . finished at about six o'clock.'

'I see.'

'She may not ask, you know.'

'Don't worry, Charles, I'll do it. Look, I must go.'

'Of course. Have a good day! And, Conrad, thanks!'

As soon as Charles had put his phone down, it rang.

'Hello?' he said. 'Charles Richards here.'

'*Charles.*' It was a woman's voice, warm and deep. 'No need to sound businesslike with me, darling.'

'Jenny, I told you not to ring me at work,' he said angrily. 'What do you want?'

'I want *you*, darling,' she answered. 'My husband has just rung. He's staying abroad for another week! So shall I expect you at 1.30 or 2.00 this afternoon, darling?'

'Look, Jenny, I . . . I can't see you today. You know that. It's impossible on Saturdays. I'm sorry, but —'

'Never mind, darling. Don't be so cross! We can see each other tomorrow.'

'I'm sorry, but I can't see you again for a while, Jenny. It's too dangerous. Yesterday —'

'What the hell do you mean?' The woman was angry now.

Charles felt desperate as he thought of her long blonde hair falling on to her bare shoulders.

'Look, Jenny,' he said softly, 'I'll explain —'

'Explain? What the hell is there to explain?' And the line went dead. Charles looked miserably at the silent phone.

~

On that day, Saturday October 6th, the death of Anne Scott was reported in a local Oxford newspaper. Many people read about it, including the Murdoch family, George Jackson, Mrs Purvis, Conrad Richards, Constable Walters and Inspector Morse. Charles also read about it, quite by chance. His wife brought home a copy of the newspaper, and left it on the table near him. He realized that she must have read the report of Anne's death.

~

The inquest on Anne had been arranged for the following Tuesday, October 9th. Constable Walters was asked to describe finding the body. The police doctor said in his report that the woman had probably died between 7.00 and 9.30 on the morning of Wednesday October 3rd, that she was perfectly healthy, and that she was 8–10 weeks pregnant at the time of death. This interesting fact caused a little surprise in the room, but finally it was decided, as expected, that she had killed herself. The case of Anne Scott was officially closed.

But that evening Morse telephoned the police doctor.

'Have a drink with me later, Max.'

'No thanks, I drink at home these days. Much cheaper.'

'Just tell me, *did* the Scott woman kill herself?'

'Morse, I only look at the body, and tell you *how* she died. It's not my job to discover *why* she died.'

'Come on, Max. I need to know the answer. Was it suicide?'

There was a long pause. The doctor clearly did not want to answer. 'Yes,' he said in the end.

Morse investigates

On Saturday October 13th, four days after the inquest, Morse interviewed most of Anne's neighbours in Canal Reach. Some of the information he received was useful, but he decided that he really needed to search Anne's house for clues. The best time would be at night, when the neighbours wouldn't see him go in.

So he went to the locksmith in Walton Street (where Walters had been, although Morse was not aware of this). He explained that he was a police inspector, and needed to get into number 9 Canal Reach (which was quite true), but that he had left his key at the police station (which, of course, was quite untrue). Unfortunately the locksmith had no key to fit the front door.

'But I *must* get in there,' said Morse. 'The truth is that the sergeant has stupidly lost both the keys —'

'You mean *three* keys, don't you, inspector?' interrupted the locksmith, going on to tell a surprised Morse about his earlier visit from Walters. Morse listened, and learned – and wondered.

'But I didn't tell the constable about the *back* door key,' continued the locksmith. 'He didn't ask.'

So two minutes and one £5 note later, Morse left the shop

with a key which would fit the back door of number 9. He hoped the locksmith wouldn't tell anyone about this, but he couldn't be sure. It was all very risky. It wasn't his case, and *risk taker* he had no good reason for being in Anne's house, especially at night. If anyone saw him . . .

It was the same morning, Saturday October 13th, that Charles Richards received the letter at his house in Abingdon. It had been delivered to the wrong address, because on the envelope was written 61 (instead of 261) Oxford Avenue, Abingdon, near Oxford. Probably the person who lived at number 61 had received it, realized the mistake, changed the number to 261, and posted it again. The envelope was clean and white, with 'Private' written at the top. The writing looked rather childish. Inside was another envelope, with 'Charles Richards' written on it. He took out the single piece of paper. It had no address, date or signature. He read:

Dear Mr Richards
I know ALL about Miss Scott who died but does Mrs Richards know? Beleive me, I could tell her everything. But you're rich, aren't you? I promise not to tell her if you give me £1000. Here's what you must do. Go to the car-park off Walton Street in Jericho. There's a big tree there with a big hole in it. Leave the money in the hole. I'll be waching you. I'll ring you soon to check. Dont try to be too clever. Remember your wife!

Although it was badly written, and the writer could not spell 'believe' or 'watching', the message was surprisingly clear. Charles read the letter several times, but remained calm. He took Celia's breakfast up to her room, kissed her lightly on the forehead and told her he was going into Oxford for the morning.

Celia Richards said nothing. As she heard him drive away, her head was full of the report she had read in the local newspaper, the report of Anne's death. She felt sure Charles had read it too. Was her husband responsible for that terrible death? She didn't even care very much any more. What she was sure of, was that they couldn't simply go on living together like this. When he came home today she would tell him, tell him everything she knew, tell him the truth. Conrad had advised her not to, but it was the only way. Oxford . . . Why was he going to Oxford this morning? He usually went to the office in Abingdon on Saturdays. Anne Scott was dead, so he wasn't visiting her. What reason could he possibly have for going to Oxford?

At the local hospital a patient was lying in bed, unconscious. A doctor was examining him.

'He's a bloody fool!' said the doctor to the nurse who was looking after the young man. 'Taking drugs is just stupid!'

'Will he be all right?' she asked.

'Perhaps, perhaps not. If he recovers, it'll be because of you, nurse, no one else.' The nurse felt pleased, and a little more hopeful than before. She was beginning to like her patient, Michael Murdoch. He was only nineteen, the same age as her. It would be so sad if he died.

That night Morse carried out his plan. He walked rapidly along Canal Reach to the canal at the end. There were no lights on at number 9 or number 10. It was just before 9 p.m., and quite dark. Turning left at the water, he walked along beside the low wall between the canal and number 9, and jumped quickly over into Anne Scott's back garden. He waited for a moment to check that the neighbours had not heard him, but all was quiet. He used the locksmith's key to open the back door. He did not dare turn on any lights, or go into the bedroom, in case he was seen, but he spent some time in the back bedroom looking through the papers in Anne's desk. Then he noticed she had a whole shelf of books by classical writers, arranged in alphabetical order. But it was strange that one of them, by the Greek writer, Sophocles, was missing.

He went downstairs and stood for a moment in the sitting room. He suddenly realized how cold it was. There was a small electric fire upstairs, but down here . . . He saw the open fireplace and moved towards it. There were still tiny pieces of burnt paper in the cold fireplace. He managed to find two pieces of an official letter. The only writing he could still read said ICH RAT. That could be German, perhaps, or part of a longer word.

Suddenly, he felt a little afraid. Here he was, in Anne's house, hiding in the dark like a thief or a criminal. Why was he behaving like this? He should have admitted immediately to the policemen investigating the case, Bell and Walters, that he had come to Anne's house on the afternoon of the day she died. It was stupid of him to feel guilty about it.

He left the house quickly, locking the back door behind

him, and got over the wall in the same way as before. But as he walked into Canal Reach, thinking he was safe at last, a heavy hand fell on his shoulder and a voice said, 'Just keep walking, will you!'

At about the same time that Morse was entering number 9, Charles Richards was driving slowly along Woodstock Road in Oxford, past the large attractive houses with their big gardens. He noticed a phone box in front of one of the houses, and wrote down the address. Satisfied, he drove away. His plan was ready.

Morse was surprised to discover that he was being pushed towards a police car, parked at the end of the street. And as he reached the car and turned round to see who had caught him, he found himself looking into the frightened face of a young constable.

'Oh, it's . . . it's you, Inspector Morse!' gasped Walters, stepping back in horror.

'Do you often arrest Chief Inspectors, constable?' asked Morse, no longer afraid, but tired and a little cross.

The two men went to Morse's flat in North Oxford, where they spent several hours, drinking whisky and sharing their information about the case. Morse admitted almost everything, but he did not tell Walters he had bribed the locksmith to give him a key to the back door of number 9. Walters confessed that he had suspected Morse of being involved in the case, and showed him the 'E.M.' page in Anne's desk diary.

'Well, young man,' said Morse finally, 'you're in a difficult position, aren't you? You find me, a Chief Inspector,

'*Just keep walking, will you!*'

in an empty house, the house where a woman has recently died. You know I have no good reason for being there. So what do you do?'

'I just don't know, sir,' said Walters miserably.

'I'll tell you what you *should* have done. You should have asked me how I got into the house. How long have you been a policeman?'

'A year and a half, sir.'

'You've got a lot to learn. Well, everything that's happened tonight, including our conversation, must be reported to Inspector Bell. All right?'

Walters agreed happily. He had been worrying about that.

'But not yet, Walters. I want to get some more information first. This case is not an easy one to investigate. Have some more whisky, and tell me about your plans for the future.' And so Walters talked eagerly, and Morse listened sympathetically. By the time the young constable was ready to leave, he had complete confidence in Morse, and was wishing he could work with him.

On his way out he remembered the question he should have asked. 'So how *did* you get into number 9, sir?' he asked.

'When you've been a policeman as long as I have, constable, you'll find it's easy to open a door without a key. You see, if it's a Yale lock, you can push a plastic card, a credit card, for example, between the lock and the door, and it opens!'

'But the lock on the back door of number 9 *isn't* a Yale, is it, sir? Good night, sir. And thanks for the whisky.'

On Monday October 15th, Mrs Gwendola Briggs, the secretary of Summertown Bridge Club, was interviewed again, this time by Morse. She was quite shocked by the difference between the two policemen. Constable Walters had asked his questions slowly and gently, but Inspector Morse had no time to bother with politeness. He asked question after question, rapidly and coldly, giving her no time to think. Who came to play bridge that Tuesday evening, the night before Anne's death? What did they talk about? Where did they sit? When did they finish? How many cars were there? So many questions! thought Gwendola.

However, she was certainly able to remember a lot, and Morse was pleased with the information she gave him. But he was still trying to remember something himself, something Anne had told him at Mrs Murdoch's party. He felt sure it was important. Perhaps Mrs Murdoch would remember.

When he rang at the door of the Murdochs' house, it was opened by a boy of about seventeen or eighteen.

'Are you Michael?' guessed Morse.

'No, I'm Edward.'

'Oh yes. Is your mother in, Edward?'

'No. She's at the hospital, with Michael.'

'Road accident, was it?' Morse had no idea why he had thought of saying that, but he noticed the boy looked uncomfortable.

'No. He's . . . he's been taking drugs. And he's . . . rather ill.'

Morse remembered that Edward was taking his exams next summer. Was he studying foreign languages? German, perhaps? Suddenly he realized. 'E.M.' . . . Edward Murdoch!

37

Wednesday afternoon at 2.30! And Anne's diary also had 'M.M.' on certain days . . . Michael Murdoch. He decided to ask a direct question.

'Were you going to have a lesson with Miss Scott the day she killed herself?' He did not take his eyes off Edward.

'Yes, that's right. But I didn't go. She told me . . . the week before that she . . . wouldn't be able to see me.'

Morse had noticed the hesitation.

'Did you like her?' he asked simply.

'Yes, I did.' The boy's voice was gentle and unafraid.

'Did she ever say anything to you about her private life?'

'No.' Now the boy seemed almost angry. Morse was puzzled.

'What about your brother? He had lessons with her too, didn't he? Did he say anything?'

'Anything about what?' Was Edward pretending not to understand? He certainly didn't want to answer.

'Never mind, boy! Tell your mother I'll come and see her sometime, will you?' And Morse stared at Edward for a few seconds, then turned impatiently away.

The note which Edward received from Anne on the day of her death, cancelling his German lesson, had been delivered to his house by hand. At the next house Morse visited, he discovered who had delivered it. Catharine Edgeley, a university student and one of the members of the bridge club, told him how Anne had asked her, late on Tuesday evening, after the bridge had finished, to post a note through the Murdochs' letter-box.

'It was addressed to Edward Murdoch?' asked Morse.

'Yes. She wrote the note at the bridge club.'

'Did she! What were you all talking about at the time?'

'Oh, I forget. The weather, work, you know, the things people usually talk about, children, that kind of thing.'

'Why didn't she give the note straight to Mrs Murdoch? She was at the bridge club, wasn't she?'

'I really don't know. Maybe Mrs Murdoch left early. I'm sorry. I don't remember.'

But at least she had remembered about the note for Edward, thought Morse. She had also told him something of great importance, but he had not realized it yet.

6

Charles Richards agrees to blackmail

The next morning, Tuesday October 16th, Morse was having his breakfast and reading a letter he had just received. It was from the Oxford Book Club to all its members, giving information about meetings and talks. Suddenly Morse stopped and stared at the letter in front of him. *We were sorry to hear of the death of Anne Scott. Although she had not been a member for long, she . . .* So he and Anne had both been members of the same club? If only he'd attended their meetings regularly, he would have seen her more often, and perhaps they would have . . . He shook his head. What was the point of wishing? It was too late now.

He looked at the letter again. It said: *Change of date – the next meeting will be on Friday 19th October, when Mr*

Charles Richards will speak to the Club on 'Owning a Small Publishing Company'. Morse wrote this information in his diary. Perhaps he would go to hear Mr Richards' talk.

When the phone rang at 10.30 the same morning, Charles Richards was in his office in Abingdon. His secretary was sitting opposite him, with her notebook. He picked up the phone.

'Richards here,' he said. 'Can I help you?'

'I'm sure you *can* help, Mr Richards,' answered a rough, uneducated voice. 'Your wife —'

Richards put his hand quickly over the phone, and told his secretary to leave the room at once. As the door closed behind her, he spoke slowly and angrily into the phone.

'Look, I don't know who you are, and I don't want to know. What you're doing is blackmail. But I believe what you said in your letter and so I'm going to pay you *one quarter* of what you asked for. Not a pound more. Understand?' There was no reply.

'And I'm not going to deliver it where you wanted. So listen carefully. Tomorrow night I'll be driving slowly down Woodstock Road at 8.30 exactly, in my blue Rolls Royce. I'll stop at the phone box at the corner of Field House Road. Then I'll pretend to make a phone call, and put a brown bag, with the money in it, *behind* the phone box. All right? It'll be safe there, don't worry about that. I'll get back in the car, and drive home. Do you understand?' Still there was silence.

'And if you try anything like this again, I'll kill you, do you hear that? I'll kill you with my bare hands!'

Finally the answer came. 'You'll be glad you did this, Mr Richards. So will your wife.' The line went dead.

As Charles Richards called back his secretary into the office, and went on working, he looked calm but his heart was banging hard under his shirt.

The members of Summertown Bridge Club had almost stopped thinking about Anne Scott by now. Old Mr Parkes was thinking about dying, which he knew would happen to him very soon. Catharine Edgeley was too busy studying to think about Anne. Gwendola Briggs, however, was looking forward to playing bridge that evening, and was pleased she had persuaded her new neighbour to take Anne's place at the bridge table. And Mrs Murdoch certainly had no time to think about Anne that night. She had just heard from the hospital that her son Michael had tried to blind himself.

Charles Richards wasn't thinking of Anne either, when he rang the secretary of the Oxford Book Club to say that he could not arrive early to meet the members before his talk on Friday. He would arrive at ten to eight, just in time to give the talk.

Even Morse did not think of Anne until late that evening, as he sat drinking beer in his local pub. He still could not remember that piece of information that Anne had given him, and he knew that after a few more beers he would never remember it.

Only Mrs Scott cried for her daughter. Alone now in an empty house, she tried to understand what could have happened. Surely she could have prevented her daughter's death, if she had known?

Next day, Wednesday October 17th, Morse was walking through the centre of Oxford, when he thought he recognized someone disappearing down a side street. It was a boy, wearing school uniform, and – yes, it was Edward Murdoch. Taking off his school tie, he went into a pub. Morse followed him.

Clearly Edward had been here before. He ordered beer and sat close to the platform at the back of the pub. Morse ordered beer too, and waited. Suddenly a girl stepped onto the platform, and the men in the pub moved closer to watch her. Soft music was playing as she slowly took off her clothes, one by one, piling them up neatly behind her. Then the music was turned off, the men clapped and the girl left the platform. She would be doing it again in five minutes' time.

'Do you want another beer?' asked Morse.

Edward jumped, looking as guilty as someone accused of stealing from a shop. But he answered, 'Yes, please.'

Morse wondered if the boy would try to run away, but Edward waited calmly for his beer. Together, drinking their beer, they watched the girl take off her clothes a second time.

'Shouldn't you be at school?' asked Morse.

'I'm free this afternoon. Shouldn't *you* be at work?'

Morse was beginning to like the boy. 'Me? I do what I want every afternoon, watch the girls, drink beer, anything. You see, I'm over eighteen. You are too, aren't you? Because of course if you're *under* eighteen, you aren't allowed to drink beer or watch girls.'

But Edward hardly seemed to be listening.

'Why did you follow me here?' he asked, frowning.

'I wanted to know why you lied to me. You told me Miss Scott cancelled your lesson *the week before* she died. That's not true. You got her note on the day of her death.'

So Edward had to tell Morse everything he knew about Anne Scott, including his brother Michael's wild stories about her. He described that time before she died when he had seen her half-dressed, the note she had sent him, and even his thoughts and dreams about her. Morse seemed to know the truth already, but he was so understanding that Edward found himself liking him more and more. Perhaps Morse was almost like a father . . . and Edward had never known his.

At 8.30 that evening George Jackson was hiding, with his bicycle, in a dark side street just off Woodstock Road. From his position he could see both the phone box and Field House Road. The light-blue Rolls Royce appeared, travelling slowly. It turned into Field House Road and stopped. The driver got out, walked round the car to open the passenger door, closed it, and, carrying a brown bag, went to the phone box.

As he came under the light of the street lamp, Jackson saw that he was a man of medium height, about forty to forty-five, with thick dark hair going grey, and dressed in an expensive suit. Suddenly Jackson went cold with fear as he saw the man in the phone box appear to speak into the phone. Was he ringing the police? The man came out, put the bag behind the phone box, and walked back to the Rolls. Jackson watched the car disappear. The road was now as quiet as the grave.

Jackson hesitated. When he had first thought of black-mailing Richards, it had all seemed so easy. Now he wasn't sure whether to take the money and go home quickly, or wait, in case someone was watching him. He waited for fifteen minutes, and then, trying to appear normal, he walked to the phone box and picked up the bag. There was no traffic, and the only person he could see was a university professor, in a long gown, crossing the road with his arms full of books. Jackson put the bag into his bicycle basket, and rode off towards Jericho.

He was beginning to feel more confident as he arrived home. After all, he had collected the money, and nobody had noticed him. He took the bag from the basket, and went inside.

But someone *had* noticed him, someone who was standing at the top of Canal Reach with a new, folding bicycle. The gown this person had been wearing, and the books he had been carrying, were now in the basket on the front of his bicycle, as he watched the door of number 10 close behind Jackson.

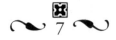

The second death in Jericho

The chairman of the Oxford Book Club was glad to see the light-blue Rolls Royce arrive in the car park. It was nearly 8 p.m., and Charles Richards was already later than expected.

*Jackson put the bag into his bicycle basket and
rode off towards Jericho.*

When Morse arrived, the talk had started. Richards was a man of medium height, wearing expensive clothes, who spoke amusingly and well. He talked of his early life as a teacher, his love of books, and his publishing company. The audience enjoyed the talk very much, and so did Morse. At the end someone asked a question.

'Were you a *good* teacher, Mr Richards?'

Richards smiled. 'I'm afraid not. I just couldn't keep control of the children in my class. In fact my lessons sounded rather like a zoo!' All the audience laughed and clapped, except Morse. He sat there, arms folded, frowning angrily at Richards. He had a feeling this man was talking nonsense.

At the bar the chairman introduced Morse to Richards.

'I enjoyed your talk —' began Morse.

'I'm glad about that.'

'Except for your last remark. I just don't believe you were a bad teacher, that's all. Someone who could keep an audience happy for an hour and a half could never be a bad teacher.'

Richards laughed. 'Perhaps I just said that to make the audience laugh.' That was possible, thought Morse. But it was also possible that Richards was lying.

'You knew Anne Scott, didn't you?' he asked.

'Yes.' Richards' voice was very gentle. 'She used to work for us.' At this point the chairman interrupted, and took Richards away to introduce him to other members. Richards left soon after.

Morse stayed on, drinking in the bar.

'Tell me about Anne Scott,' he said to the chairman.

'Oh yes, poor old Anne! She had a lot of ideas for the club. It was her idea to persuade Charles Richards to speak to us, you know. In fact, she arranged it all with him.'

Morse suddenly felt excited. Anne and Charles Richards! Now he was beginning to understand. The clues were all there, like pieces of a puzzle. It must have been Charles who was visiting Anne the day she died. Morse had seen the light-blue Rolls Royce, with a parking ticket on its window, parked at the top of Canal Reach that day. And now he even remembered what Anne had told him at Mrs Murdoch's party – she had said that she used to travel a lot with Charles Richards, sometimes on business, sometimes for pleasure. She and Charles must have been very close.

Just then he heard the police and ambulance sirens outside. Not again! How long ago had Charles Richards left? A quarter of an hour, perhaps. He ran to the public phone in the bar, but the sergeant at the police station told him Inspector Bell had been called to investigate a murder.

'Got the address, sergeant?' asked Morse.

'Just a minute, sir. I've got it here somewhere . . . It's one of those little streets down in Jericho . . . It's –'

But Morse had put down the phone several words ago, and was on his way to Canal Reach.

'What's happened, Walters?' he said as he entered number 10.

'It's Jackson, sir. He's been killed. Someone phoned us. He didn't give his name, just told us Jackson was dead.'

'When was the call?'

'About 9.15, sir.'

'Are you sure of that?' Morse was puzzled. He went

47

upstairs to find Jackson's dead body on the bed. He had died from wounds to the head, and was lying in a pool of blood.

'He died between 7.30 and 9 p.m., I'd say,' said the police doctor, after examining the body.

'Can't you be more accurate, Max?' asked Morse. 'If you asked me, I'd say he died between 7.15 and 7.45.'

The doctor smiled. 'Nobody *would* ask you, Morse. But if you want to bet on it, I'll be more exact. Between 8.15 and 8.45.'

'How much will you bet on that?'

'£10?' The two men shook hands on their bet.

As the doctor left, Inspector Bell was looking worried.

'Who would have killed an ordinary little man like Jackson?' he asked, scratching his head. 'Why? How? Any idea, Morse?'

But Morse didn't reply. Poor old Bell, he was thinking. And he, Morse, knew all the answers. He knew exactly who had murdered Jackson, when and why.

Just then Walters came into the room to report to Bell.

'This is what Jackson did earlier this evening, sir. At 5.30 he bought some bread from a local shop, at 6.45 he repaired Mrs Purvis's toilet, and at 8.05 he —'

'*What?*' cried Morse.

'At 8.05 he went to the pub on the corner —'

'Nonsense!' shouted Morse.

'But he *did*, sir! He was *there*! He was drinking beer there, and finally left at about 8.20.'

Morse was so shocked that he had to sit down quickly. Had he got it all wrong? Because if Jackson was drinking beer after 8 p.m., while Charles Richards was talking to the

Oxford Book Club about publishing, Charles could not possibly have killed him.

'You'd better get that £10 ready to give the doctor!' said Bell, laughing at Morse's unhappy face.

∼

The next morning Morse phoned Charles Richards at home.

'Have you heard about the trouble in Jericho, sir? A man was murdered there last night.'

'Really?' The line was bad. Richards' voice wasn't clear.

'His name was George Jackson, and I think you knew him, sir.'

'I'm afraid you're wrong. I don't know anyone in Jericho.'

'But you used to, didn't you?'

'Pardon, Inspector?' Was he pretending not to hear?

'You knew Anne Scott – you told me so.'

'Anne – yes, I knew her. But I didn't know where she lived.'

'You were – very friendly with her once? You were close?'

'Yes, that's right,' said Richards quietly. 'But I never visited her in Jericho. Look, Inspector, I loved her very much once, but, well, our affair came to an end.'

'Where were you on the afternoon of Wednesday October 3rd?'

'I can remember where I was, but I really can't tell you, Inspector . . .'

'Were you with another girlfriend, perhaps?'

'Well, yes.'

'Wasn't your car parked near Canal Reach that afternoon?'

'It certainly wasn't! You can't prove that!'

Morse hesitated. 'Well, let's forget that for the moment,

49

sir. But I must ask for your, er, friend's phone number.'

When Morse rang the woman, Mrs Jennifer Hills, to check Charles's alibi, she told him she had been in bed with Charles for most of that day, from about 11.30 a.m. to after 5 p.m. So perhaps Charles *had* been telling the truth about that. She sounded rather attractive, thought Morse. Perhaps he would interview her later.

Morse and Lewis in charge of the case

Later that day Bell asked Morse to come into his office to discuss Jackson's murder.

'You were right about the weapon, Morse,' said Bell. 'Someone must have hit Jackson several times and then knocked his head on the bed post. That's what killed him.'

'I thought so,' said Morse. 'The doctor said it was a weapon with a square edge, and Jackson was lying close to the bed post. Could it have been an accident?'

'It was bloody deliberate. So why do you think someone wanted to kill him, Morse?'

'Perhaps someone was looking for something in his house.'

'We've searched the whole place. He had all kinds of tools . . . well, he did odd jobs for his neighbours, didn't he?

'He did some birdwatching too, didn't he? There was a pair of binoculars in his bedroom.'

'Well, I suppose he used to watch birds along the river when he went fishing.'

'I think he used to watch Anne Scott in her bedroom opposite. No curtains at her bedroom window, were there?'

'Dirty little man!' said Bell. 'By the way, Morse, it's strange that you just happened to be in Jericho at the time of both deaths.'

'Just chance. Have you interviewed the people who saw Jackson in the pub last night?'

'Yes. Jackson was certainly there till about 8.20.'

Morse frowned. Charles Richards seemed to have the perfect alibi. But that just made Morse even more eager to investigate it. What about the phone call to the police? Someone had wanted to make sure the police knew when Jackson died – and give Charles Richards an alibi at the same time.

'Morse,' said Bell rather desperately, 'have you got *any* ideas about this case?'

Morse decided to tell him everything he knew, starting with his evening with Anne Scott and finishing with his phone call to Jennifer Hills. He even told Bell about bribing the locksmith to hand over a back door key for number 9.

'If you can help me to solve this case,' said Bell quietly, 'I'll be grateful – you know that, don't you?'

'I'll do my best,' answered Morse. 'I'll think a bit about it. I'm sure there's a clue missing somewhere.'

The police found very little further information about Jackson. He had hardly any family or friends. But someone had entered his house between 8.30 and 9.00 that Friday evening, argued with him, and killed him. That person had also searched all the drawers and cupboards. The neighbours had been too busy watching television to notice anything.

'The two deaths must be connected, sir,' suggested Walters.

'That's bloody obvious!' said Bell.

Although his boss was clearly tired and depressed, Walters felt he had to mention something else.

'Did you know, sir, that there wasn't a single book in Jackson's house?' But Bell wasn't listening.

Old Mr Parkes, one of the members of the bridge club, felt very happy that day. A neighbour had discovered it was his birthday and brought him a cake to celebrate. It had been years since anyone had remembered his birthday. And then he remembered – birthdays! That's what they'd been talking about at the bridge club the evening before Anne Scott's death. And the police had asked him to tell them everything he could about that night, so he rang up the police station at once.

'I see, sir,' said Bell. 'Very interesting. Birthdays, was it? Thank you very much, sir.' He smiled to himself as he put the phone down. What a useless piece of information!

Bell didn't know it at the time, but soon he wouldn't have to worry about the case of the Jericho deaths any more. Morse was surprised to discover that the Assistant Chief Commissioner had decided to remove Bell from the case.

'Bell's a good man,' the ACC told Morse later that day, 'but he's not the most intelligent policeman in the world. I'm going to put *you* in charge of this case, Morse.'

'I wouldn't want to take a case away from Bell . . .'

'Don't worry about that, Morse,' said the ACC. 'He'll be getting promotion soon anyway.'

Promotion, thought Morse. *He'd* like that too. But promotion usually meant spending more time in the office, and he knew he was happier out in the street solving crimes.

'You're the best man to solve this Jericho case,' said the ACC. 'And you can have Lewis as your assistant.' For the first time that afternoon Morse looked happy.

Lewis had become a policeman at the age of twenty, and then worked hard to receive promotion to sergeant. Six years ago he had started working with Morse on murder cases, and although Morse had often been very difficult to work with, Lewis felt proud to be the great man's colleague and friend. At the police station people even spoke of them as a team – Morse and Lewis. But now Lewis was feeling disappointed. So far in the case of the Jericho deaths Lewis had not been asked to help Morse at all. He could not understand it.

As he was eating his breakfast the phone rang. It was Morse.

'Lewis? I want your help.'

'My help, sir? I'm afraid I'm busy today at the station —'

'Forget all that! The ACC says you're assisting me with this Jericho case. I need your help.'

Suddenly Lewis felt warm and happy. He was needed!

'I'll be glad to help, sir. When do you want me?'

'Now, of course! Hurry up and finish your bloody breakfast!'

'Right, Lewis,' said Morse when the sergeant arrived in his office. 'Tell me, if I get a parking ticket, what do I do?'

'Well, sir, there's an office where you should go and pay the fine immediately. The officials there receive a copy of the parking ticket, and they also keep details of who paid the fine, and when it was paid.'

'Very good, Lewis! I didn't know all that. Now I've got your first little job all ready for you.'

At about mid-day Lewis returned with the information that a parking fine for a blue Rolls Royce, parked on the corner of Canal Reach and Canal Street at 3.25 p.m. on Wednesday October 3rd, had been paid by cheque on Friday October 5th, in the name of Mr C. Richards, of 216 Oxford Avenue, Abingdon.

Morse was delighted. He rang Charles Richards' office.

'I'm sorry, Inspector,' explained the secretary, 'but Mr Richards is at lunch. Could you ring again tomorrow?'

'Tomorrow?' repeated Morse. 'Doesn't he work in the afternoons?'

'Mr Richards works very hard,' said the secretary coldly, 'But I think he – er, has a meeting today.'

'Oh, I see,' replied Morse. 'Well, that's obviously much more important than helping a police investigation.'

'I could *try* to contact him.'

'Yes, you could – and I hope you will,' said Morse quietly.

Ten minutes later Charles Richards rang.

'Sorry I wasn't in when you rang, Inspector. Can I help?'

'Yes, you can, sir. There are one or two things I'd like to talk to you about. It's better not to discuss them on the phone.'

'As you wish.' Richards didn't seem to care.

'Tomorrow? At about 10 o'clock? At your office?'

'That's fine.'

'Can I park outside your office?' Morse asked innocently.

'You can, Inspector. So difficult parking a car these days, isn't it?' Richards sounded just as innocent.

It was early evening in one of the Jericho pubs.

'Poor old George!' one drinker was saying to another. The tall man in the corner lifted his head and listened carefully.

'George Jackson, you mean?' the second man said.

'Yes, you know, the little man who was murdered in Canal Reach. Didn't have many friends, did he?'

'No, he liked being alone. Good at fishing, he was.'

'Good at watching the girls too, I hear! Used his bloody binoculars to look at the woman opposite, didn't he?'

'And he had a bit of money too, you know. Last Thursday I saw him paying £250 into his post office account —'

As more people came into the bar, the conversation became more difficult to hear. The tall man in the corner got up and left the pub. Lewis thought he had gathered enough information about Jackson to keep Morse happy.

Mr and Mrs Richards

Next morning Morse drove from Oxford to Abingdon, and parked in front of Richards Brothers Publishing.

The secretary showed him straight into Charles Richards' office.

'Good to see you again, Inspector,' said Richards.

But Morse said sharply, 'You lied to me, sir, about your visit to Jericho on Wednesday October 3rd. I want to know why.'

Richards looked at him with what seemed real surprise and answered, 'But I *didn't* lie to you. As I told you —'

'Your car had a parking ticket in Jericho that afternoon. So someone *else* must have been using your car, is that right?'

'I . . . suppose so, yes. But —'

'And you paid the fine two days later. So someone stole your chequebook, did they, sir?' Richards was looking very uncomfortable but Morse continued. 'Of course I realize it must have been someone else, because you yourself have an alibi for that afternoon. I checked with the young lady, Jennifer Hills —'

Richards waved his hand wildly from side to side, as if rubbing words off a board. 'Stop, er, please don't mention her name! I don't want anyone else to be involved in this.'

'I'm afraid she is already involved, sir. She has given you a perfect alibi. Now all I want to know is who drove your car to Jericho that afternoon.'

Richards said miserably, 'Oh, Inspector, I should never have lied to you.' He shook his head. 'I never thought you'd know about the parking ticket. You police discover everything! Let me tell you the truth. Anne and I had an affair while she was working for the company. When we went away on business trips, we used to book into hotels as husband and wife. I mean, I never intended to divorce my wife or anything.'

'Did your wife know about it?'

'No, I honestly don't think so. Anyway after a while, our affair just didn't seem so exciting any more, and Anne decided to leave the company. But last summer my brother and I moved our company to Abingdon, and Anne and I met again by chance, and well, I started visiting her, usually one afternoon a week.'

'Did you have a key to her house?'

'Key? Er, no, I didn't.'

'Was the door unlocked on the afternoon we're talking about?'

'Unlocked? Er, yes. It must have been, mustn't it?'

'Tell me exactly what you did, sir.'

Richards seemed to be trying to remember. He wasn't looking at Morse. 'I went in and called her name. She didn't seem to be there, so I went upstairs.'

'Upstairs?' Morse asked.

'Yes.' Richards smiled sadly, then looked squarely into Morse's eyes. 'To the back bedroom . . . Look, you know all this anyway, don't you?'

'I know almost everything,' said Morse simply.

'We usually had a glass of wine or something there before we . . . we went to bed, in the front bedroom.'

'Wasn't that a bit risky, sir, going to bed together in daylight?'

Richards looked puzzled. He was taking a long time to answer.

'Ah, I see what you mean!' he said suddenly. 'Someone

could see us through the bedroom window. It's strange, isn't it, that Anne never bothered to put curtains at the windows?'

Richards had cleverly avoided that particular trap, thought Morse, but he could easily fall into the next one.

'I waited for about twenty minutes, realized something must have happened to delay her, and just left.'

'You didn't look into the kitchen?'

'No.'

'Had it started raining when you left, sir?'

'*Started?* I think it had been raining all afternoon. When I arrived I left my umbrella just inside the front door.'

'Just on the right of the door as you go in, you mean?'

'I'm not sure, Inspector, but wasn't it on the *left*, just behind the door?'

'No, no, you're quite right, sir. I was just testing you, that's all. Now I know you really were there. Somebody else saw your car that afternoon, went into the house, and saw your black umbrella by the door, and your dark-blue raincoat by the stairs. So that proves you were there, doesn't it?'

'Yes. I should have told you the truth at once —'

'You still haven't told me the truth!' shouted Morse.

'What!' gasped Richards.

'You're still lying to me! The truth is that you weren't in Jericho at all that afternoon!' Morse stood up. 'The person in Anne Scott's house that day was certainly not wearing a dark-blue raincoat! You've been lying from the beginning —'

'But I *haven't* been lying!' Richards was holding his head in his hands.

Suddenly they heard a quiet voice behind them.

'Yes you have, Charles! You've been lying all your life. You've lied to me for years about everything, we both know that. The strange thing is that now you're lying to *save* me!' The woman who Morse had thought was the secretary entered the room and sat on the edge of the desk, crossing her long slim legs and turning to Morse. 'I'm Celia Richards, Charles's wife. My dear husband didn't want his normal secretary, who may be another of his girlfriends,' she added bitterly, 'to know about the police coming here, so he asked me to be his secretary for today. I've listened to every word you've said, and I think it's time to tell the truth now. You were trying to trick Charles, Inspector, by mentioning the dark-blue raincoat. I know that because, you see, it was *me* who went to see Anne Scott that afternoon, and I was wearing a brown leather jacket, which I can show you if you like. Have you got a cigarette, Inspector?'

Celia continued her story, smoking one of Morse's cigarettes, as the two men listened. Morse believed every word of it.

'I never really knew about the affair between Charles and Anne until the day I happened to visit Charles's office when he was away, and found a letter from Anne to him. When I read it I discovered he had been visiting Anne recently. She wrote that she needed to see him, that she was in desperate trouble and needed money. She mentioned that she had kept all his letters to her, and that she would use them to force him to help her, if necessary. I decided I would visit her myself, so on Wednesday October 3rd, when Charles was out, I took the Rolls to Jericho, parked it (with difficulty!),

'Yes, you have, Charles! You've been lying all your life.'

and found number 9 Canal Reach. The door was unlocked, so I went in. The house seemed quite empty. I found the letters in the back bedroom upstairs. Just then someone came in and shouted Anne's name from downstairs! I was so frightened! I just stood there trembling. As soon as I heard the person leave I left too. I found a parking ticket on the Rolls, so I paid the fine two days later, using my own cheque (C for Celia, Inspector!). It was only later, when I read the newspaper report, that I realized I had been in the house while Anne was hanging dead in the kitchen. I decided to tell Charles everything. He insisted on trying to protect me. It all seems so stupid now, lying to the police! I can't think why we decided to do it.'

'Thank you very much, Mrs Richards,' said Morse after a moment's silence. 'I'll contact you again if I need any information from either of you.'

As he drove away, Celia stood watching from the window. Finally she turned to the man in the armchair and broke the long silence between them.

'He's clever, you realize that, don't you?'

'I'm not sure. Do you want a drink?'

'Yes.' She stared at the street again. She'd told only one big lie, but she'd felt almost sure that Morse had noticed it. But perhaps he wasn't as clever as she thought.

10

Some hidden clues

At lunch-time Sergeant Lewis told Morse what he had discovered about George Jackson. He had certainly not been poor. He must have earned quite a lot of money from the odd jobs he did for his neighbours, because he owned his house, had nearly £2000 in his post office account and fishing equipment worth about £1000. Nobody seemed to like or dislike him, they just weren't interested in him. How sad to live and die like that, thought Lewis.

Morse then repeated Mrs Richards' story to his colleague.

'Did you get a statement from her, sir? No? Well, I'd better go and interview her again, hadn't I?' Lewis thought it was strange Morse had forgotten that.

'All right, Lewis, go and see her this afternoon.'

In fact the inspector seemed to have lost interest in the Richards family. At 3.40 that afternoon he was at number 10 Canal Reach again, although he didn't really know why.

The little house was dirty and poorly furnished. Downstairs Morse noticed an information sheet called 'Moving'. Wasn't that the television programme for people who could not read or write? Was Jackson like that? Perhaps that explained why there were no books in his house. What a difference from number 9, where Anne had books, by classical writers mostly, all round the house! If Jackson could only have seen . . . But he *had* seen. He'd almost certainly seen more than he should have done, of the woman who took her clothes off in front of her uncurtained window.

Morse went up to the front bedroom again, to see how much Jackson could have seen. He picked up the binoculars and looked at the house opposite. You could see everything from here! It was almost like being *in* Anne's bedroom. Then he went to the back bedroom and, opening the window, looked into the garden. Suddenly he gasped with excitement. *Someone was searching for something in Jackson's shed!*

He ran downstairs, opened the kitchen door and rushed out. Unfortunately the man must have heard him opening the window, and all Morse saw was a man disappearing over the low wall separating number 10 from the canal. It was getting dark, and Morse didn't feel brave enough to chase the man on his own.

He went into the shed. It was full of fishing equipment and garden tools. There was a new fishing rod against the wall. Morse looked around helplessly. Who had been so eager to search the shed? And why? Morse had no idea.

Before leaving Canal Reach, he crossed the road to number 9 and went in. There was a brown envelope just inside the front door. Probably a bill, thought Morse, and put it in his pocket.

He drove through Jericho to Walton Street, past the signs on some new buildings: Doctors Green and Smithson, the Jericho Testing Laboratory, Barclays Bank . . . But he didn't notice them and therefore missed the hidden clue.

Lewis had returned from Abingdon. He had interviewed Celia Richards alone at the house, and showed Morse her statement.

'There are some spelling mistakes here, Lewis,' said Morse. 'And make sure the address is correct.'

Lewis said nothing. He knew his spelling wasn't very good.

'And how much do you think that new fishing rod of Jackson's cost?' Morse asked suddenly.

'I don't know, sir. It's a modern one, light and hollow. Very strong, too.'

'I asked you how much it cost, not how bloody fantastic it was!' Lewis had often seen Morse like this. Usually it meant that he was cross with himself about something, but usually, too, it meant that he was getting closer to the truth.

At 9.30 that evening Charles Richards flew to Madrid.

The next morning Morse and Lewis started looking through all the information that Bell had collected on the two Jericho cases.

'Which case shall we look at first, sir?' asked Lewis.

'How the bloody hell do I know, man?' Morse didn't have much hope of finding new clues in the boxes of papers in front of him, but somehow he had to discover what connected the two deaths.

'Why do you think she killed herself?' he asked suddenly.

'She was pregnant, wasn't she?'

'But you can get rid of a baby these days, can't you?'

'Some women would be very unhappy about that.'

'Do you think she knew she was pregnant?'

'I'm almost sure she knew. Eight to ten weeks pregnant at the time of death, the doctor said. And my wife knew then, that *she* was pregnant, sir.'

'Did she?' Morse did not seem very interested.

'Although she wasn't exactly sure until the laboratory sent the result of her pregnancy test back —'

Morse jumped to his feet, his eyes shining with delight, and shook Lewis by the shoulders. 'Lewis, you're bloody wonderful!'

'Really?' replied Lewis, looking puzzled.

'Look in the boxes! There's an envelope – see what's in it!'

Lewis stared at the words ICH and RAT on the pieces of burnt paper in the envelope, and still did not understand.

'Only yesterday I drove past the building, Lewis! And I'm such a fool I didn't notice! Don't you see? The JerICHo Testing LaboRATory! They must have tested her, and then they wrote to tell her she was pregnant —'

'But she probably *knew* she was having a baby. It wouldn't have made her kill herself.'

'Ye-es.' Morse sat down, a little disappointed. 'But perhaps that was the day she received the letter from them . . . Lewis! Ring up the laboratory and ask when they wrote to her. And ask the postman when he delivers the post to Canal Reach —'

'The post arrives there at about 7.45 in the morning, sir.'

'Does it? Eight to ten weeks! How long has Charles Richards been in the Oxford area? Three months, I think! Just ring him up, will you, and ask —'

'Wait a minute, sir! Which one shall I ring up first?'

'It doesn't bl—' But Morse stopped himself and smiled kindly at his assistant. 'Ring up whichever you like, my dear Lewis.'

He was still smiling sweetly as Lewis started phoning. This was the clue he had been waiting for.

Lewis discovered that Anne had been worried enough to visit the Jericho Testing Laboratory on Monday October 1st to ask for news. A letter had been sent to her the next day, informing her that she was in fact pregnant, and it had probably been delivered to her house by 8.30 on Wednesday morning, the day of her death. And Conrad Richards told Lewis that Richards Brothers Publishing had indeed moved to Abingdon three months before.

As Morse listened happily to this information, Lewis picked up a small piece of paper which had dropped on to the floor.

'It says "Birthdays", sir. The old man at the bridge club remembered they were talking about birthdays the night before Anne died. That's not much help, sir, is it?'

Morse, however, sat without moving, his forgotten cigarette still smoking between his fingers, his eyes staring straight ahead of him.

∾'

After talking to Lewis, Conrad phoned Charles in Spain.

'The police wanted to know how long we've been in Abingdon.'

'Was that all? I see,' said Charles slowly. 'And Celia?'

'She's fine. She's gone to Cambridge to stay with her sister Betty for a few days.'

'Good,' answered Charles. Things were going very well.

∾'

In fact Celia was worried and unhappy. As she drove to Cambridge, she thought bitterly about the last two weeks.

66

How awful her life had suddenly become! It had all started so long ago, when she first met the Richards brothers. Of course she had immediately fallen in love with Charles. But she had always known that he had a hard side to his character, and that he was far too interested in other women. After their wedding they had been happy for several years, but she had always suspected him of having affairs. Now she knew it was true, because he had admitted it. And Conrad? Would she have been happier if she had married him? She could have done – he loved her as much as Charles did – but he never seemed as exciting, as strong, as ambitious as Charles. The brothers looked very similar, but had quite different characters.

When she arrived at Betty's, and saw her sister's kind face, she found she could not stop crying, 'I'm sorry,' she whispered, 'you see, I can't tell you about it, Betty, but I've done something terribly wrong.'

11

Morse and Lewis discuss the case

At lunch-time that day in the pub, Morse drank beer as usual, while Lewis ate a large plate of egg and chips.

'Beer's good for the brain, you know, Lewis,' said Morse.

'You may be right, sir, but I need a bit of solid food to keep going. Do you think we're anywhere near solving the case?'

'We're doing well, my old friend. We have all the main facts now. Anne Scott went to a bridge evening, and there

I'm sure she discovered something which added to her problems. She wrote a note to Edward Murdoch, cancelling his Wednesday lesson. In the morning she received a letter from the Jericho Laboratory. She burned the letter and she – hanged herself.

'Now remember, Jackson had been repairing her garden wall. He went to her house to collect his tools, using the key she lent him. He entered the kitchen and found her hanging there. By accident he knocked over the chair and put it back near the door. Now just think, Lewis. *Anyone* in that situation would have rung up the police immediately. So why didn't Jackson? There was no reason for the police to suspect him of murder. I think in fact he was the person who rang us up later. I'm sure he *found* something in the kitchen, Lewis, something he was too greedy to leave there. It was probably a letter she'd written that he took, and in his hurry to get out of the house, he forgot to lock the door. That confused us, didn't it. You see, Anne must have locked her front door every night, then taken the key out and put it in the sitting room. Then he went home and read the letter —'

'But you told me he *couldn't* read!'

Morse pretended not to hear this. 'Either the letter was written to the police, or to the man she loved most in her life, Charles Richards. And Jackson was planning to blackmail him. But what happened next at number 9? Celia Richards went in during the afternoon. Jackson must have seen her, as he saw *me* later, but he didn't know she was Charles Richards' wife. But he *did* realize he'd forgotten to lock the door, and as soon as Anne's house was empty he crossed the road and put his key through her letter box.

That's how it happened, Lewis, I'm sure of it.'

'Yes,' said Lewis slowly, finishing his last chip. 'In fact I decided some time ago that's what happened.'

'Really?' said Morse. 'Well, I expect your rapid brain will have already discovered how the two deaths are connected.'

'Well, yes, sir. We suppose Jackson succeeded in blackmailing Charles because he was seen taking £250 to the post office the day before he died. Perhaps Richards gave him the money, then followed him home, and came back next day to kill him and get Anne's letter back.'

Morse shook his head. It *could* have happened that way, but it *hadn't*. 'You're wrong on one point, Lewis. *It wasn't Charles Richards who murdered Jackson*. He was giving a talk, with me in the audience, and he never left the platform! The police found Jackson's body while Charles was still talking to the Book Club.'

'Perhaps he asked someone else to get the letter back?'

'Carry on, I'm interested.'

'His wife? His brother?' suggested Lewis.

'I don't think his wife would be strong enough to hit Jackson like that. But brother Conrad? I think it's time we talked to him. You go and see him this afternoon.'

'I could get his fingerprints and compare them with the ones we found in Jackson's house,' said Lewis eagerly.

'Right. And while you're doing that, I'll interview Charles's girlfriend, I think. What's her name?' Morse asked innocently.

'Jennifer Hills, sir.'

Lewis decided he liked Conrad Richards. He seemed a quiet,

pleasant man, and gave his fingerprints willingly.

'Now, sir, can you tell me where you were between 8.00 and 9.00 on the evening of Friday October 19th?'

Conrad shook his head. 'I can't, I'm afraid. Probably at home reading, but I really can't remember.'

'You live alone, sir?'

'That's right. I really don't think I can produce an alibi.'

'Never mind, sir. Not many people can. Just one more thing. Could I speak to your brother?'

'He's in Spain on business, for about a week.'

'Oh! Well, we'll see him when he gets back.'

After Lewis had left, Conrad sat silently for a moment. Then he picked up the phone.

Morse, however, was unlucky. According to her neighbours Jennifer Hills was also in Spain.

'Look, sir,' said Lewis. 'We must get Conrad's fingerprints checked at once. I think Charles must have asked Conrad to help him get Anne's letter back. Charles gave the talk while Conrad visited Jackson. Perhaps Conrad never meant to kill him.'

'Perhaps,' said Morse. He was not convinced. Conrad did not seem the kind of person to attack an old man so violently. But how could he judge? He hadn't even met Conrad. He should have interviewed him that afternoon instead of chasing women.

'We're going back to see Conrad again, Lewis! Yes, now!'

But Conrad was no longer in his office. According to his secretary, he had left in a taxi, with two suitcases. Morse was very angry with himself for letting Conrad escape. He demanded the secretary's keys, and together he and Lewis searched the brothers' offices. It was Lewis who found the blackmail letter locked in Charles Richards' desk.

On their way back to Oxford, Morse read the letter again and again. He looked more and more puzzled.

'You know, Lewis,' he said when they were back at the police station, 'I think we've got the wrong idea about this case.'

'Really, sir? I think Conrad's fingerprints will solve it.'

'Don't bet too much money on that,' said Morse.

Lewis left his boss staring miserably into a cup of cold tea, and, whistling happily, went to get the fingerprints checked. Poor old Morse, he thought. A clever detective, but, well, who had found the blackmail letter? And who had thought of the fingerprints? It wasn't a very difficult case after all. You didn't need a great brain to solve a murder case, just careful investigation of the facts. As soon as the fingerprints at Jackson's house were proved to be Conrad's, police would be sent to all the main airports, and he would be caught.

But half an hour later Lewis discovered that *the fingerprints did not match*.

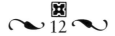

A difficult time for the Murdoch family

E dward Murdoch felt cross and tired as he rode home on his bicycle from school. His football team had lost their match that afternoon, and he still had school work to do for the next day. Everything seemed to be going wrong recently. Even the traffic in Oxford was worse than usual. He was getting hungry too, and hoped his mother had cooked something good for a change. In the last ten days they had eaten nothing but fish and chips or chicken or eggs. Of course he knew he shouldn't blame his mother too much – she spent a lot of time visiting Michael in hospital, and was obviously very worried about him – but Edward felt *he* was having a hard time too.

So when he arrived home, he threw open the kitchen door and asked aggressively, 'What's for supper?'

'I thought we'd have some fish and chips —' His mother was ironing one of his shirts.

'Fish and chips! Not again!'

Suddenly his mother put down the iron, and dropped onto a chair at the table. Her shoulders were shaking and tears were running down her face. She looked completely helpless. Edward had never seen his mother like this, or ever imagined that such a solid, dependable person could become so desperate and lose control so badly. He immediately forgot his own problems and remembered how much he loved her.

'Don't cry, Mum! Please don't! I'm sorry, I really am . . .'

He put a hand on her shoulder as she tried to dry her eyes.

'I haven't helped you much lately, have I?' he said quietly.

'It's not that. It's . . . just that I can't manage . . . I've tried so hard. I just don't know what to do!'

'It's Michael, isn't it, Mum?'

'Yes, I went to see him today. The doctor says he's lost the sight in one eye completely . . . and they don't really know . . .'

'You mean, he'll be *blind*?'

'The doctors are doing their best but . . .'

'We mustn't lose hope, Mum.'

'How did we get into this awful situation!' she cried desperately. 'If only your father hadn't died!' And if only they had never decided to adopt . . . She would keep her guilty secret for ever – she knew she would never be able to love Michael as she had always loved Edward.

At the hospital the doctor was slowly removing the bandage from Michael Murdoch's head. He took off his watch and held it in front of his patient's left eye.

'How are you now, Michael?'

'All right. But I feel a bit tired.'

'Have you any idea what time it is?' He was still holding his watch in front of the boy's staring eye.

'I don't know. Tea-time, is it? About 5 o'clock?'

The watch said 8.45, but the boy's injured eye stared past without seeing it. As the doctor put the bandage back, he shook his head sadly at the nurse waiting anxiously beside the bed.

Next morning, in Morse's office at the police station, Morse and Lewis examined the blackmail letter.

'His spelling's even worse than mine, isn't it, sir?'

'You mean Jackson, I suppose?'

'Well, yes. Who else could have written it?'

'I don't know yet. But I'm sure *he* couldn't have written it. You know, he used to watch that television programme for

'I don't know. Tea-time, is it? About 5 o'clock?'

people who can't read or write. I think he persuaded someone to —'

'But it's a terrible letter! That's why I think he wrote it!'

'Well, you're wrong, Lewis! Look at it! I agree the spelling's bad, but the *message* is very clear! It's a good letter, because it communicates what the writer wants to say.' Morse banged on the table. 'No! *Jackson did not write that letter*. And another thing, if he *had* written it, wouldn't he have asked for a lot more money?'

'Perhaps he did, sir, and Richards refused.'

'Ye-es. You may be right. I hadn't thought of that. Lewis, go and interview the woman at the Jericho post office, Mrs Beavers, isn't it? Ask her if Jackson could read or write. He'd have to sign his name to pay in money or get it out of his account. And ask her about the odd jobs he used to do for neighbours, will you?'

When Lewis returned, he had to admit Morse had been right.

'He could only just sign his name, sir. Mrs Beavers often had to read official letters to him. And she said his most recent job, before Anne Scott's wall, was some electrical work for Mrs Purvis at number 7.'

'Interesting, Lewis. That could be an expensive job. Let's visit Mrs Purvis. And remember, the person who wrote that letter was well educated enough to *pretend* to be uneducated. I wonder if Mrs Purvis went to a good school?'

To Lewis, this question seemed the strangest that Morse had asked so far, and he was still puzzling over it as the police car arrived at Canal Reach.

As soon as he met Mrs Purvis Morse knew she hadn't

written the letter. There wasn't a serious book anywhere in her sitting room. She wasn't what he called a well educated person.

'We'd like to know more about Mr Jackson, Mrs Purvis. He did some electrical work for you, didn't he?'

'Yes, that's right.'

'Would you mind telling me how much he charged you?'

'Er . . . £75.' She sounded almost guilty, thought Lewis.

'Not at all expensive,' said Morse. 'Did you ever do any little jobs for *him*?'

Mrs Purvis looked surprised. 'What do you mean . . . I . . .'

'Mr Jackson couldn't write very well, could he? Did you ever write a letter for him?'

'No, Inspector, I didn't.'

'But did you ever *read* a letter for him?'

This was clearly a shock for poor Mrs Purvis. The muscles in her face trembled. She opened her mouth but no words came out.

'It's all right,' said Morse gently. 'I know all about it, you see, but I'd like to hear it from you, Mrs Purvis.'

So the frightened woman told them the truth. 'Jackson was charging £100 for the electrical work, you see, but, well, I haven't got much money, and he was willing to accept £75 if I would just read a letter to him and keep it a secret. And of course it was only after beginning to read it to him that I realized it must have been a letter left by Anne Scott on the kitchen table before she hanged herself. Mr Jackson took the letter away after I'd only read about half of it. There were four pages of writing. It was a kind of love letter, and it said the man she was writing to was the only

76

one she'd ever really loved, and that he shouldn't blame himself in any way. I just can't . . . can't remember any more.'

'You didn't do anything else for Jackson?' asked Morse.

'No, honestly, I didn't. That was all.'

'You didn't even find a telephone number for him?' Morse spoke calmly, but now Mrs Purvis broke down completely. Her shoulders shook and tears ran down her face as she replied.

'I didn't, but I did explain to him how to find someone's phone number. I didn't suspect then that he was going to blackmail anyone!'

'Never mind, my dear,' said Morse kindly, putting a hand on her shoulder. 'We understand, and we're going to forget all about it. But can you remember anything at all about this man Miss Scott was writing to? Did you see the envelope, with his name on it?'

'No, I'm sorry, I didn't.'

'She must have written his name somewhere. "Dear" somebody? It wasn't "Charles" by any chance, was it?'

Mrs Purvis smiled happily through her tears, pleased to be helping the police at last. 'Yes, it was. "Dear Charles." That was how she started the letter!'

That evening Morse visited Michael Murdoch in hospital. Unfortunately the boy was asleep so Morse could not speak to him. He started reading the information attached to the bed (Name: Michael Murdoch, date of birth: October 2nd . . .), but was thinking about something else, and did not notice one of the final clues to the mystery of the Jericho deaths.

In fact, that night, it took him four hours of careful thought, and several whiskies, to solve the first part of the problem, and discover the name of the man who killed Anne Scott.

Next morning he sent Lewis out to find certain information.

'You were right, sir,' said Lewis when reporting back to Morse. 'The other driver in the road accident which killed Anne Scott's husband was *Michael Murdoch*.'

'And why didn't that fool Walters tell us that? He investigated Anne Scott's past, didn't he?'

'Perhaps he didn't think it was important, sir.'

'I see,' replied Morse coldly. 'And I suppose you, with your wide experience, would agree with him?'

'Well, yes, sir. It didn't seem important at the time.'

'I'm disappointed in you, Lewis. If you're ever going to be a good detective, you'll have to realize that it's these tiny details that solve cases in the end.'

'Why are you angry with me, sir? What have I done wrong?'

'I'll tell you, Lewis. Your reports are bloody careless! Look at the mistakes in this statement taken from Celia Richards!'

Lewis looked down and said nothing. He knew his spelling was bad, and that he had written reports and typed statements in a hurry recently. He often had to work late into the night so that he could give Morse the reports in the morning.

'Sir, that's not fair. You don't realize —'

'Look at this!' continued Morse, waving the statement. 'And I particularly asked you to check Mrs Richards' address! What the hell's the use of a sergeant who can't even get an address right? And another thing —'

But Lewis was no longer listening. This wasn't just unfair, it was *wrong*. Perhaps he wasn't as clever as Morse, but he knew his facts. So he waited patiently until Morse became calmer.

'The address on Mrs Richards' statement is correct,' he said slowly and simply.

Morse's mouth opened – and closed. 'You mean, Lewis, that she lives at *261*? But this letter here, with a cheque to pay the parking fine, is from C. Richards, *216* Oxford Avenue, Abingdon.'

There was a moment's silence. It was Lewis who spoke first. 'This means that it wasn't Celia but *Conrad* Richards who paid the fine, sir. 216 is his address.'

Suddenly light flooded Morse's brain. His eyes were shining as he jumped up. 'I've got the answer to the whole problem, Lewis! Let's go and have a drink, to celebrate!'

'No, sir. Before we go anywhere, I want to know about all my other mistakes —'

'Nonsense, Lewis! Nothing to worry about! They're excellent reports!' He put his arm round Lewis's shoulder. 'What a team we are, you and me! We're bloody fantastic!'

'So you think you've solved the case, sir?'

'I *know* I have, my old friend. I not only know who killed Anne Scott, but I also know who killed George Jackson. You want the names? Shall I tell you now?'

So Morse gave the two different names. Lewis was very puzzled by the first one, which was completely unknown to him, and very surprised by the second.

13

The story of Oedipus

'There are three ways of explaining events in human lives,' began Morse, as he and Lewis sat drinking in the pub. 'One explanation is that everything just happens by chance. Another is that we ourselves make things happen, according to our characters. And the third explanation is that we can't influence what's going to happen to us in any way, because the future has already been decided by God, or the gods, or fate, or whatever people call it. That's what the Ancient Greeks believed, you know.'

'What do *you* believe, sir?'

'Me? Well, I certainly don't believe in fate. But it's quite clear that Anne Scott did. She even mentioned it to me that evening – when I met her – and she had shelves of classical books in her house. There was one missing from her bookcase, written by Sophocles. I found it on her desk. She must have been reading it very recently.'

'I don't really understand, sir —'

'Well, let me tell you a story. Once, a long time ago, a young man called Oedipus, who didn't know who his parents were, visited a strange town and fell in love with the beautiful, lonely queen, Jocasta, who lived there. Her husband the king had died recently, so she and Oedipus married and had several children. They could have been very happy, but in fact their story is one of the most horrible in the whole of Greek writing. You know what happened to them, of course?'

80

Lewis looked sadly down at his beer. 'I'm sorry, sir, I don't. I didn't get much of a classical education at my school.'

Morse looked kindly at his assistant. He knew why he liked working with him. He was such an honest, sincere man, not proud at all. Morse continued more gently. 'It's a very sad story. Oedipus finally discovered that it was he himself who had killed the king, without knowing it, and that the king had been his own father! So he had married his own mother, and they had had children together! When the queen discovered this, she hanged herself, and Oedipus blinded himself. That's the story of Oedipus, as told by Sophocles.'

Morse told the story so well, thought Lewis. If his teachers had been able to make things as interesting as that, he would have learnt a lot more at school.

'So you see, Lewis,' Morse continued, 'how this story connects with our case. Anne married a man and they had a baby, but they couldn't keep it, so it was adopted. That's a modern way of getting rid of a baby. The Greek king and queen had left their baby son Oedipus on the mountain to die. That was *their* way of doing it! Now, Lewis! What would every mother remember about her baby, even if she gave it away when it was only a few hours old?

'At the bridge evening, the night before she died, they were talking about *birthdays*. Old Mr Parkes told Bell that. *That's* what no mother ever forgets, when her only baby was born! Well, I think someone who knew the Murdochs must have mentioned to Anne that night that Michael Murdoch was adopted. And then Mrs Murdoch herself probably told Anne that Michael's birthday was that day, October 2nd! Fate was cruel to Anne.'

'I thought you didn't believe in fate, sir.'

Morse went on without answering. 'The king had been killed while travelling, and Anne's husband died in a road accident! I think she knew the other driver was Michael, but after all it was an accident – she didn't blame him for it. He even came to her for private lessons in German, and I think they must have been rather interested in each other, as they sat close together at the small desk in her back bedroom, a beautiful, experienced woman and a strong young man. They must have had sex. And then she thought she was pregnant. She wrote to Charles Richards, the only man she'd ever really loved, asking for help, advice and perhaps money. Celia Richards read that letter, and we don't know whether Charles replied or not. I imagine Anne felt very alone. She couldn't talk to Michael about it – he was too young to know what to do. She began to think she had failed in everything, a broken marriage, an unwanted baby, an affair with a married man, and then Michael Murdoch . . .'

Morse stopped speaking. He seemed to be in a dream. Lewis brought more beer to their table.

'So,' continued Morse, without bothering to thank Lewis for the beer, 'Anne thought she'd never meet a really nice man to spend her life with. The younger ones were already married, and the older ones, like me, were no use to her. So she began to think that fate was against her. She had been reading the Oedipus story recently, and suddenly, when they were talking about adopted children and birthdays at the bridge evening, she realized the terrible truth. *Michael*

Murdoch was her own son. He was a modern Oedipus. Everything fitted. Her husband had been killed in a road accident by her son, a son who she had been having sex with, and who had made her pregnant. Fate wanted her to die. She felt she wasn't strong enough to fight against fate, and so, my old friend, she chose Queen Jocasta's death and hanged herself. And strangely enough, Michael Murdoch blinded himself, just as Oedipus did. So, as I told you, Lewis, the one man guilty of Anne Scott's death was Sophocles.'

The beer glasses were empty again. Morse passed a £5 note to Lewis. 'You've been too generous recently. *I'm* paying this time.' What a surprise, thought Lewis. But he had a question to ask.

'Do you still think fate is nonsense, sir?'

'Of course I do!' replied Morse crossly. 'Bloody rubbish! It's just chance, all of it! Do you know, Lewis, I feel like some egg and chips? What about you?'

Another surprise, said Lewis to himself. 'I do too, sir.'

'But you'll have to pay for mine. I haven't any money left.'

〜

It was 7.30 in the morning, and Charles Richards was lying awake in bed in a Spanish hotel, smoking. Next to him lay Jennifer Hills. He found himself thinking, not of the beautiful woman beside him, but of his wife Celia. She had looked so sad and hurt when she had learnt of his affair with Anne. He was also thinking of his brother Conrad, who had rushed to Spain the day before to talk to Charles. Why hadn't he kept calm and stayed in England? The police couldn't suspect Conrad of anything.

That afternoon Celia received a phone call from Inspector Morse. 'Yes, Inspector,' she replied to his question, 'my husband will be back from Spain soon. In fact he phoned me just now, to say he'll be flying back on Monday morning.'

'Could I see him then, Mrs Richards?'

'Yes of course, Inspector. 3 o'clock at our house?'

'Fine. Have you any idea where your husband's brother is?'

'Conrad? No idea at all. On a business trip somewhere, but nobody knows where, I'm afraid.'

Lewis came into the office as Morse was finishing his phone call. He noticed how pleased his boss looked.

'3 o'clock on Monday, Lewis! We'll get him then! I'm looking forward to it, aren't you?'

'Sir, I'm afraid I've got some bad news.' Morse looked up sharply. 'You're not going to like this, sir, but Anne Scott's baby son was adopted by a London couple and died before his third birthday. So Michael Murdoch couldn't be her son.'

Morse stared at his assistant. If that was true, then the story of Oedipus did not explain Anne's death.

But in fact Morse was very close to the truth. The final clue to the mystery was the unopened letter which he had picked up from just inside number 9 Canal Reach, and which now lay in his jacket pocket.

On Monday afternoon Morse arrived at Charles Richards' large house, number 261. In the double garage was a Rolls Royce, a smaller car and a folding bicycle. The Richards greeted him, hand in hand. Morse watched them carefully. They looked a perfect couple, surprisingly happy together.

Or did they just want to make him think that?

'I'll leave you two to discuss whatever it is you want to discuss,' said Celia.

'She's obviously glad to have you back, sir,' said Morse, as Celia walked out of the sitting room.

'I think she is, yes,' answered Richards. 'But I hope you haven't come here to talk about my personal life?'

'I'm afraid your personal life is very much involved in this case, sir. Do you mind if I smoke?' said Morse, offering the packet to Richards.

'Not at all. But I won't have one at the moment, thanks. Look, let's get on, shall we? It's about Anne Scott, isn't it?'

'Among other things, yes. For example, do you know where your brother Conrad is?'

'No idea at all, I'm sorry.'

'Did he ring you – while you were in Spain?'

'Yes, Inspector, he did. He told me your man had taken his fingerprints. Why was that?'

'Because I suspected him of murdering Jackson.'

'*Conrad*? You can't suspect *him*! Do you want *my* fingerprints?'

'No. You see, you've got a very good alibi for that night. *I* watched you giving that talk all evening. No, I know exactly who killed Jackson, and it wasn't you.'

'Well, that's something, I suppose.'

'Did Conrad also tell you we found the blackmail letter in your desk?'

'No, but Celia did. It was stupid of me to keep it.'

'But I'm glad you did. It's the biggest clue in the case. And Jackson didn't write it!'

'*What?*'

'No. It couldn't have been him because he couldn't write.'

'But he rang, Inspector! It must have been Jackson!'

'Try and remember exactly what he said. Did he mention the letter? How can you be so sure it was him?'

'Well, to tell the truth, Inspector, I have a special reason for knowing it was him. You see, I decided to change the time and place for leaving the money, so that I could follow him. And he came to the place I described, so I know it was him.'

'How much money did you take? Where did you arrange to meet?'

'I took £250, and left the money behind a phone box at the corner of Field House Road, off Woodstock Road.'

'So you took Conrad with you? How did he follow Jackson home? On his bicycle?'

'What the hell are you talking about, Inspector? I followed Jackson in the car —'

'There's a folding bicycle in your garage, sir. Look, I don't think either you or your brother murdered Jackson, but I've got to solve the murder, and I must have the truth!'

'Well, you're right, Inspector,' admitted Richards quietly. 'We put the bicycle in the back of the car, and Conrad used it to follow Jackson home to Canal Reach. He wore a gown and carried a few books, to look like a professor, so that Jackson wouldn't suspect anything.'

'And then what happened? You knew Jackson's address.'

'Nothing happened, Inspector.'

'You didn't drive Conrad into Jericho the night you were giving the talk at the Oxford Book Club?'

'No, *I didn't!*'

'Where was Conrad that night?'

'I honestly don't know. Probably at home. He says he just can't remember.'

'But *you* can remember what you did that night, sir?'

'I drove straight home after the talk, and arrived home by 10.30, I think. But why don't you ask my wife?'

'It doesn't really matter what time you arrived home, sir. Thank you, you've been most helpful.' Morse stood up to go. 'We'll have to have a statement, of course. I can send Sergeant Lewis along whenever it suits you.'

'Can't we do it now, Inspector? I'm very busy in the next few days.'

'No hurry, sir. It's not really important. But it's funny, you know, people's memory of events often changes when they start to write it down. Strange, isn't it?'

'I don't like what you seem to be saying,' said Richards, his voice hard and cold.

'No? Well, I'm only saying that it's a good thing to have time to think about what happened. Perhaps you could give your statement to Sergeant Lewis sometime next week?'

'Monday? Will that be all right?' By now the two men were standing at the open front door, and Lewis, waiting by the police car, could see them clearly.

Morse walked down the road to join Lewis. 'Well?' he said.

'You were right again, sir.'

Morse sat back happily as they drove away. 'Things are going well, Lewis. Now we just wait for the fish to bite!'

Lewis, waiting by the police car, could see them clearly.

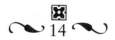

14

Morse solves the case

On Tuesday evening, after Edward Murdoch had visited his brother in the hospital, he was surprised and a little worried to be shown into a room where Morse and Lewis were waiting for him. There were no polite greetings.

'Can you spell "believe"?' asked Morse sharply. The boy looked unhappy but before he could answer, Morse threw the blackmail letter across the table at him. 'Of course you can! You're well educated. No! Don't touch the letter! The fingerprints on it are important. The person who wrote it couldn't spell "believe", or was pretending he couldn't!'

There was a long, uncomfortable silence.

'Did you write it?' asked Morse. 'Or did your brother?'

The boy shook his head. 'You must be joking!'

Lewis whispered something to Morse, who appeared to agree. Picking up his pen and notebook Lewis went out. There was silence in the room. Morse spent the next ten minutes reading a magazine which had been lying on the table. Edward began to look more and more worried. Finally he could stay silent no longer.

'What's happening? You must tell me!'

'We're waiting for Sergeant Lewis to come back.'

'How long will he be?'

'It depends. Some people help the police in their investigations, others don't,' answered Morse, turning a page.

'He's gone to ask Michael some questions, hasn't he? It's

not fair! Michael's ill! He shouldn't be disturbed!'

'I'm sorry, young man,' said Morse very gently and quietly, 'but Sergeant Lewis and I are trying to solve a murder. If people help us, then we can discover the truth. If they don't, then sometimes we have to do things we don't like doing.'

'But I've *told* you, Inspector. I didn't write —'

'You're lying!' said Morse sharply.

Just then Edward did a very strange thing. He put both his hands deliberately on the letter in front of him, and sat back, looking pleased with himself.

'That's not very clever,' said Morse. 'Now you'll have to explain why you did that. You'll have to tell me the truth. The sergeant'll be back in a moment with your brother's statement, then you'll sign one. Then I'll ring your mother. She'll be worried about you by now. You're all she's got, and she's had a hell of a time these last few weeks, hasn't she?'

Edward could not bear any more. He put his head in his hands, and cried. Morse quietly left the room and called in Lewis, who had been sitting just outside all the time, reading a newspaper.

So Edward told them the whole story. He'd seen Anne's letter to Charles on her desk in the back bedroom, ready to post, and he had read it. In it she had begged for advice and money. She was sure she was pregnant, and the father could only be Charles, because she had had sex with no one else. Even if he could no longer be her lover, she needed him as a friend. She still had all his letters and she would burn them, if only he would help her. If he didn't help, she just didn't know what to do.

How sad, thought Morse. That was the letter Celia found in Charles's office. And what reply did Anne get? Probably a letter from Charles saying he couldn't help her.

'So I told Michael all about it,' went on Edward, 'and you see, he was always desperate for money for drugs, so he suggested blackmailing Charles. We wrote the letter together and sent it. But next day Michael was taken to hospital, and I – well, I felt frightened of what we'd done. I never rang up Mr Richards, or went to the tree to see if any money had been left there. I'm really sorry.'

While Morse and Lewis were still at the hospital, two policemen, waiting at Gatwick airport, walked up to a middle-aged man with greying hair who had just arrived from Madrid.

'Mr Conrad Richards? I arrest you for the murder of Mr George Jackson of 10 Canal Reach, Jericho . . .'

Morse decided to interview the accused man alone next morning.

'Good morning, sir. We haven't met before, have we? I've met your brother several times of course.'

'Charles has told me about you, Inspector. I think you'd better explain why you've arrested me.'

'Oh, I was hoping *you* were going to explain it all to *me*. Well, I think this is what happened. Charles told you about the blackmail letter he received. You agreed to help him, and when he went in his Rolls Royce to leave the money behind the phone box, you went with him, and then followed the man who took the money. You used Charles's folding bicycle.'

'It's all true, except that I have my own folding bicycle.'

'Ah well! Even the best of us make mistakes sometimes.'

'I think you're about to make a big one, Inspector. Go on.'

'That Friday Charles took you with him when he went to speak at the Oxford Book Club. You visited Jackson and —'

Richards shook his head. 'No, Inspector. Listen to me a minute! Perhaps you're right in thinking Charles meant to go and see Jackson, frighten him a little. My brother is capable of doing that, believe me! But you see, something happened to prevent that – *Jackson was murdered*. We just didn't need to worry about him any more. I certainly didn't go to his house that night. But I'm afraid I haven't got an alibi, as you know.'

'You see, sir, the person who killed Jackson was looking for something, a letter from your brother perhaps. I saw a man running away from Jackson's shed. Was that your brother? Or you?'

'Jackson's *shed*? Look, Inspector, I know I have no alibi but I want to know what proof you have against me.'

'Well, you see, there were several fingerprints in Jackson's bedroom, and you remember that my sergeant took yours.'

'Yes, he did! And I know that my prints won't match anything there, because I've never been in the bloody house, never!'

'I'm sorry, sir, you see, Lewis is a good policeman but he's just not very good at fingerprints. Perhaps you wouldn't mind letting him take yours again? In fact he's waiting outside now.'

Richards sat down heavily on the chair, his head between his hands. He appeared completely exhausted.

'Cigarette?' offered Morse. Richards took one.

'When did you discover the truth?' he asked very quietly.

'Discover that you weren't Conrad Richards? Well, now . . .' and Morse, as he smoked, told the story to the man *whose real name was Charles Richards.*

'So tell me how you solved the case, Morse,' said the Assistant Chief Commissioner that afternoon.

'Well, sir, the first important clue was discovering that it was Anne who arranged to invite Charles to the Oxford Book Club to talk about publishing. Nobody else in Oxford knew the Richards brothers – they had only moved to the Oxford area a few months before. The only person who knew them was Anne, and she was dead. So they carried out the same plan as earlier in the week, when it was in fact *Conrad* who drove the Rolls to Oxford, and *Charles* who followed Jackson to Canal Reach. This time Conrad agreed to give the talk that Charles had already prepared, while Charles visited Jackson. I don't think Charles intended to murder Jackson, just frighten him and get Anne's letter back, the letter Anne had left for him before hanging herself, but unfortunately Jackson's head hit the bed post. That killed him. Now Charles had to act quickly. He realized that Conrad, pretending to be Charles, must be given a solid alibi, so he rang the police to tell them Jackson was dead, and left.'

'He didn't find the letter?'

'He says he didn't, and I think he's telling the truth.'

'What about the change of date for the talk? Was that deliberate?'

'I don't think so. I think Charles just wanted to take his girlfriend Jennifer to Spain with him, and she couldn't manage the first date, that's why he changed it. But it was lucky for the brothers, because it meant the audience was small, and there was less chance of someone recognizing Conrad. Then after that they realized they had to go on pretending, so Charles told Celia everything, even about his affair with Anne, and asked her to help.'

'So how did they manage to make you think Conrad was Charles? You interviewed them both!'

'Yes, sir, but the point was that Lewis and I had never been *together* when we'd met Conrad, and we'd never met the brothers when *they* were together. I saw the man I thought was Charles speaking at the Book Club. I spoke to the real Charles next day on the phone, but the line was bad, so I didn't realize it was a different person. The next time I rang him, he was out, but he must have asked Conrad to ring me back. The next day I had arranged a meeting with him, so Celia had to act as secretary and Conrad played the part of Charles. There was an important clue I missed that time – Celia asked me for a cigarette, but if the man with her had really been Charles, she would have asked *him*, because he's a heavy smoker. Then Lewis went to get Conrad's fingerprints. If I had gone with him, I'd have recognized Conrad as the man who was pretending to be Charles. But I was . . . er . . . busy somewhere else. Conrad's fingerprints matched nothing in Jackson's house, because it was *Charles* who had been there. Another clue I missed was that Charles's office was full of cigarette ends, while Conrad clearly doesn't smoke at all. Then we made our final visit to Abingdon, when Celia and Conrad again acted as husband and wife. But by now I suspected the truth, so I managed to get Conrad to the front door, so that Lewis could recognize him as Conrad, not Charles.'

'But why didn't you arrest him immediately?'

'Because, sir, I didn't want the big fish to escape. Lewis knew the real Conrad, so I told Conrad (acting as Charles) that Lewis would take a statement from him, knowing the real Charles would have to come back for this. Conrad phoned his brother to tell him to return from Spain at once. It was a trap.'

'And they arrested him at Gatwick airport?'

'Yes. As soon as I told him Lewis was going to take his fingerprints, he knew it was the end. They would match the ones in Jackson's house, you see. Then I offered him a cigarette . . . and that was that. He confessed to Jackson's murder.'

'I suppose, by the way, that his fingerprints *did* match?'

'Well, actually, no, sir. I'm afraid I must have been a bit careless myself when examining Jackson's room —'

The Assistant Chief Commissioner stood up, shocked.

'Morse! Don't tell me . . . they were . . .'

Morse looked guilty. 'I'm afraid so, yes, sir. *They were mine.*'

The case of the Jericho deaths was solved, but Morse was still worried about the answers to two questions. The first problem was that the story of Oedipus didn't quite explain

Anne's death, now that Lewis had discovered Michael Murdoch wasn't her son. The second was that although he felt sure Charles had written a letter to Anne, that letter had never been found. That Wednesday morning, she must have received a letter from the laboratory informing her she was pregnant, and one from Charles refusing to help her. That was why she killed herself.

But if she only decided to kill herself on Wednesday morning, why had she cancelled her lesson with Edward, the evening before? Another strange thing was that her bed had not been slept in. But perhaps she *did* go to bed, got up early, and made the bed. But why would she get up early? Usually she stayed in bed late on a Wednesday, after her bridge evening.

'Morning, sir!' Lewis came cheerfully into Morse's office.

'You're bloody late!' said Morse. 'Come on, we're going to Jericho again, Lewis. We're looking for that letter from Charles Richards, replying to Anne's. It *must* be there. I know you've all looked for it, but I think I can find it.'

'Right, sir,' said Lewis quietly.

As the police car turned into Walton Street, Morse noticed a shop selling fishing equipment. An idea came to him.

'Jackson was buying his fishing rod from there, wasn't he?'

'That's right, sir.'

In Canal Reach the two men walked towards the canal and climbed over the low wall into Jackson's back garden. Morse opened the door of the shed, and found the new rod. Carefully he looked inside it.

'You see, Lewis? It's hollow inside. Just the place to hide a letter, don't you think?' But although he went on searching, there was no sign of anything hidden in the rod.

'Never mind, sir, it was a good idea,' said Lewis. 'Shall we go and have a beer in the pub, to celebrate solving the case?'

Morse looked surprised. Lewis was not usually the one to suggest a drink. 'All right,' he agreed. 'But I still want to find answers to those two questions.'

In Canal Reach again, Morse looked up at the front of Anne's house. Still no curtains at her bedroom window.

'I wonder . . .' he said slowly. 'Have you got the key to number 9? Just go in and see if she had an alarm clock in her bedroom, would you?' They opened the front door together, and there inside the door was a long brown envelope. It looked like a gas bill, but, more important than that, it reminded Morse of the other brown envelope he'd picked up from that same place ten days before, and forgotten about till then. Now he pulled the first envelope out of his jacket pocket and read the letter inside.

Summertown

C U R T A I N • C O M P A N Y

Summertown Curtain Co.
South Parade
Summertown
Oxford

8th October

Miss A Scott
9 Canal Reach
Jericho
Oxford

Dear Miss Scott,
I am sorry there has been a problem with
the new curtains you ordered from us. We
were therefore unable to fit them as you
requested on Wednesday October 3rd. I am
now able to inform you that they are
ready.
Please contact me to arrange another date
for fitting them.
Yours sincerely,

J. Burkitt

J. Burkitt (Manager)

So she cancelled Edward's lesson because she was expecting
men from the curtain company to fit the new curtains! And
she got up early to let them into the house. But they didn't
come. The post arrived instead, and life became too much
for her to bear.

'Here's the alarm clock, sir,' said Lewis, coming downstairs,
'set for 7.45. So she did get up early. And you know that
letter from Charles that we've been looking for? Perhaps she
burnt it with the letter from the laboratory. We'll never find
it now.'

'Perhaps not,' agreed Morse. 'He hasn't admitted writing to her, you know.'

'Well, I can understand that. He's already responsible for one death.'

'I don't think he cares about what he did to Jackson, Lewis. But I don't think he'll ever forgive himself for helping to cause Anne's death.'

In the pub Lewis offered to buy the drinks.

'You sit down, and just read that, sir,' he said, giving Morse a rolled up letter. 'I came to Jericho early this morning, and found it hidden in Jackson's new rod in the shed. I'm sorry I didn't tell you before, but it isn't the letter you were looking for. I haven't read it, sir.'

The name on the envelope was *Inspector Morse*. Morse read the single page of writing.

Dear Inspector Morse,

Perhaps you have forgotten me. We met once at a party where you had too much to drink and were very nice to me. I hoped you would contact me – but you didn't. Please, be kind again now and deliver a letter for me, without reading it. I know what I'm going to do is selfish, but I just can't bear life any more.

Anne Scott.

Inside the first envelope was another envelope, opened, addressed to Charles Richards.

'You haven't read this either, then, Lewis?'

'No, sir. But obviously that's the letter Jackson found in Anne's kitchen, and asked Mrs Purvis to read to him.'

'I think I'd better do what she asked. Make sure Charles Richards gets this letter as soon as possible, Lewis.' Charles would be deeply hurt by that letter. But he, Morse, had been hurt too. 'I hoped you would contact me – but you didn't.' Oh! If only she'd known . . . if only she'd known how much he wanted to . . .

He felt Lewis's hand on his shoulder and heard his kind voice saying, 'Don't forget your beer, sir!'

Jericho has not changed much since the events described in this book, although Canal Reach is no longer on the map. Instead of the old narrow houses where Anne Scott and George Jackson died, there are modern flats, and Mrs Purvis lives in one of them. But Mrs Beavers still works at the Jericho post office, and the locksmith keeps his shop open in Walton Street.

Losing the sight of one eye did not stop Michael Murdoch studying at university, and Edward did well in his school examinations. The bridge club managed to find some new members, although old Mr Parkes was buried on the day that Charles Richards was found guilty of the murder of George Jackson. Surprisingly, Constable Walters left the police and joined the army. Sergeant Lewis became a father, and celebrated by having a bottle of wine with his favourite egg and chips.

'*You sit down, and just read that, sir.*'

And Morse? He still goes to his local pub most evenings. In December he was invited to another party in North Oxford, and as he waited in the queue for the food, his eyes rested for a moment on the slim, attractive shape of the woman in front of him. But he said nothing, and after eating his meal alone, he left early and walked home.

GLOSSARY

account money kept in someone's name at a bank or post office

admit to say that something is true, to confess

affair a sexual relationship with a man or woman

alibi proof that a person was in another place at the time of a crime

alphabetical following the letters of the alphabet, e.g. A, B, C

attractive good-looking

bare *(adj)* with no clothes on

bear *(v)* to suffer pain or unhappiness

blackmail *(v and n)* to demand money from somebody in return for not telling secrets about them

bet *(v and n)* to risk money on the result of something, e.g. a race

binoculars special glasses for seeing the details of distant objects

blonde golden or yellow-haired

bloody a swear-word

brain the part of the head that thinks and remembers

bridge a card game

call (on call) available to help colleagues if necessary

case a criminal or legal matter, often involving a trial

chairman the head of a club or the person in charge of a meeting

classical the best music of an earlier time

constable a policeman

convince to persuade someone into believing something

darling a word used when speaking to someone who is loved

exams, examinations school or university tests

fair just, right

fate destiny, an unseen power deciding our future

fine *(n)* money paid as punishment for parking in the wrong place

fingerprints marks made by fingers which can be used as proof
fishing rod a long piece of metal or plastic used for fishing
fold *(v)* to bend something so that it takes up a smaller space
gown a long black dress, worn by some university professors
hang (oneself) to kill oneself by hanging with a rope around the
    neck
hell (What the hell . . .?) a word used to express anger or surprise
inquest a legal investigation into the cause of a sudden death
interrupt to break into another person's conversation
laboratory a place where scientists do tests
locksmith someone who makes and sells keys and locks
odd jobs small repair jobs in the house and garden
parking ticket an official notice, usually put on a car, ordering
    someone to pay a fine for parking in the wrong place
poetry creative writing in verse, usually expressing deep feelings
pregnant expecting a baby
professor an important university teacher
promotion getting a more important job
publishing printing and selling books
Reach a small street
recover to get better after an illness
representative *(n)* an agent of a company, who sells its products
sergeant a police officer below the level of an inspector
sex (to have sex) to make love
shed a small wooden building in a garden where tools are kept
siren a device that makes a long, loud sound as a warning
slim with an attractive figure; not fat
spell *(v)* to write words without making mistakes
statement information given to the police, written down
suicide *(n)* killing yourself

The Dead of Jericho

ACTIVITIES

Before Reading

1 Read the information on the back cover of the book. Which of these statements are facts (F), and which are guesses (G) that may or may not be true?

1 A woman called Anne was found hanging from her kitchen ceiling.

2 She kicked the chair away herself, after tying the rope round her neck.

3 She died while Chief Inspector Morse was drinking in a pub.

4 Morse met Anne while she was alive.

5 Anne was one of Morse's closest friends.

6 The police discovered Anne's dead body.

2 Read the story introduction on the first page. Inspector Morse is different from other policemen. Can you guess how this shows in his working life? Circle Y (Yes) or N (No) for each idea.

1 He often drinks in pubs when he should be working. Y/N

2 He is sometimes too drunk to think clearly. Y/N

3 He goes to classical concerts when he should be working. Y/N

4 He doesn't concentrate hard enough on his job. Y/N

5 Female suspects can easily persuade him they are innocent. Y/N

6 Other policemen don't like working with him because of his weaknesses. Y/N

7 He doesn't expect people to do the right thing all the time. Y/N

8 He doesn't believe in punishing people for every single mistake they have made. Y/N

While Reading

Read Chapters 1 to 4, and then answer these questions.

Who ...

1 ... gave the party where Morse met Anne Scott?
2 ... entered Anne's house on the afternoon of October 3rd?
3 ... watched Anne's house from across the road?
4 ... seemed to have an unhappy marriage?
5 ... had been having private German lessons with Anne?
6 ... was the man Anne had married?
7 ... was looking after Anne's spare door key?
8 ... did Walters suspect was the 'E. M.' in Anne's diary?
9 ... promised to give Charles Richards an alibi?

Read Chapters 5 to 7. What do you know about the case so far? Decide which of these statements are facts (F), and which are guesses (G). Explain why you think this.

1 George Jackson wrote the blackmail letter to Charles Richards.
2 The pieces of burnt paper in Anne's fireplace were part of a longer letter written in German.
3 'E. M.' in Anne's diary referred to Edward Murdoch.
4 Anne sent a note to Edward cancelling his German lesson because she was planning to commit suicide.
5 Jackson took the blackmail money left at the phone box.
6 Charles Richards visited Anne's house on the day she died.
7 Anne was pregnant with Charles' baby.
8 Jackson was murdered between 8.20 and 9 p.m.

Before you read Chapter 8, which of these opinions do you agree (A) or disagree (D) with, and why?

1   Anne committed suicide.
2   Anne was murdered.
3   Anne had threatened Charles that she would tell his wife that she, Anne, was pregnant with his child.
4   Charles Richards could not possibly have killed Anne Scott or George Jackson.
5   Jackson was killed because he knew too much.
6   Celia, Conrad, and Charles Richards were all involved in both of the Jericho deaths.

If *you* were Inspector Morse, what action would you take next?

Read Chapters 8 to 10. Choose the best question-word for these questions, and then answer them.

Who / What / Why

1   . . . was the 'murder weapon' that killed Jackson?
2   . . . seemed to have the perfect alibi?
3   . . . did Walters notice when he searched Jackson's house?
4   . . . had the Bridge Club members been talking about, on the evening before Anne's death?
5   . . . had paid the parking fine for the blue Rolls Royce?
6   . . . didn't Charles want Morse to mention his girlfriend's name?
7   . . . was it risky for Charles and Anne to go to bed together in daylight, in Anne's house?
8   . . . was pretending to be Charles' secretary?
9   . . . did Charles Richards lie to Morse at first?
10   . . . informed Anne that she was pregnant?

Before you read Chapter 11, think about the clues so far, and the possible developments. How would you answer these questions?

1 What two pieces of information convinced Morse that Celia was telling the truth?
2 Is it possible that Charles *had* been in Anne's house, and that Celia is lying to protect *him*?
3 Celia said she found Anne's letter to Charles (see page 59). Did Charles reply to it, and if he did, what happened to the letter?
4 Celia told Morse 'only one big lie' (see page 61). Can you imagine what it was?
5 What might be hidden in Jackson's shed?

Read Chapters 11 to 13. What do we learn in these chapters about the following?

1 the last letter Anne wrote
2 Anne's door keys
3 Conrad's alibi
4 Michael Murdoch
5 the blackmail letter

6 Mrs Purvis' confession
7 John Westerby's road accident
8 the Richards' address
9 the story of Oedipus
10 Charles and Conrad Richards

Before you read Chapter 14 (*Morse solves the case*), can you guess the answers to these questions?

1 What did Morse mean when he said, 'Now we just wait for the fish to bite!' (see page 87)
2 Who wrote the blackmail letter to Charles Richards, and why?
3 Who killed George Jackson, and why?
4 Why did Anne cancel Edward Murdoch's German lesson?
5 How and why did Anne Scott die?

After Reading

1 Here is the report of Anne's death which appeared in the local newspaper. Choose one suitable word to fill each gap.

The Oxford Herald   *Thursday 4th October*

WOMAN FOUND HANGED IN JERICHO

Last night a woman was found _____ in her kitchen at 9 Canal _____, in the heart of the Jericho _____ of Oxford. The woman's name was _____ Scott. She was 36, and lived _____. Students often visited her at her _____ for private lessons in German.

A _____ call was received at the central _____ station at about 9.15 yesterday evening, _____ them to go to Canal Reach. _____ the police arrived, they found the _____ door unlocked and Ms Scott's body _____ from the kitchen ceiling. She had _____ been dead for about ten hours. _____ appeared to have been stolen.

Our _____ spoke to Chief Inspector Bell, who _____ the body and who is in _____ of the investigation into Ms Scott's _____.

'At this stage we have no _____ to suppose any other person is _____,' said Inspector Bell. 'There were no _____ of forced entry, and at the _____ we believe Ms Scott's death to _____ a simple, if tragic, case of _____. It is possible that she had _____ some bad news recently, and we _____ like to talk to anybody who _____ have further information about this. Our _____ will continue until we are completely _____.'

Police are trying to get in _____ with Ms Scott's friends and private _____, who may be asked to give _____ at the inquest.

2 Here is Morse's report on the case. Put the seven parts of the report in the right order. Start with number 2.

1 Conrad Richards agreed to pretend to be Charles and give the talk at the Book Club, while Charles visited Jackson to get Anne's suicide letter. Although Charles probably didn't intend to murder Jackson, they must have had a fight, and Jackson fell and hit his head on the bed post, which killed him.

2 Anne Scott discovered she was pregnant and wrote a letter to Charles Richards, the father of the baby, asking for help, but he wrote back, refusing her request.

3 Michael and Edward Murdoch knew Charles Richards was having an affair with Anne Scott, as Edward had seen Anne's letter to Charles in her house. Michael persuaded Edward they should send a blackmailing letter to Charles.

4 The brothers kept up their pretence of being each other, to maintain Charles' alibi, but in the end Lewis and I saw through it, and Charles confessed to killing Jackson.

5 That afternoon, George Jackson used the key she had given him to enter her house. He saw her dead body in the kitchen, and it was probably him who moved the chair. He found her suicide letter and took it away with him.

6 However, when Michael was taken to hospital, neither he nor Edward followed up their blackmail letter. It was Jackson who, knowing nothing about this letter, made a blackmailing phone call to Charles Richards. And when Jackson collected the money, Charles followed him home to see where he lived.

7 When she received his reply on October 3rd, together with confirmation of her pregnancy from the laboratory, she hanged herself.

111

3 **On the day of Anne's death, Celia Richards went to Anne's house (see page 59). Later, she told her husband Charles about it. Complete Charles' side of the conversation.**

CELIA: Charles, there's something I must tell you.

CHARLES: _____

CELIA: You're always going out! No, it can't wait! It's important!

CHARLES: _____

CELIA: Well, Charles, I went to Jericho today.

CHARLES: _____

CELIA: *I* don't, but *you* do. Or knew her, I should say. In fact, you knew her rather too well.

CHARLES: _____

CELIA: Oh, don't play games with me, Charles! You know who I'm talking about! Anne Scott! The woman who was found dead! The woman you were having an affair with!

CHARLES: _____

CELIA: It's no good you lying to me! The other day when I was in your office, I saw a letter she'd written to you!

CHARLES: _____

CELIA: Yes, exactly, *that* letter. Well, when I read it, I decided to try and get your letters back, the ones you wrote to her. So I took the Rolls and drove to her house.

CHARLES: _____

CELIA: Well, I just pushed open the front door, and walked in.

CHARLES: _____

CELIA: No, the house seemed quite empty. I found the letters upstairs – I've burnt them, by the way – but Charles, the worst thing is that I was in the house while she was hanging, dead, in the kitchen!

112

4 Here are extracts from four letters in the story. Who wrote them, and who read them? Choose from the names below (you will need two names more than once). What effect did the letters have, and what happened to each of them in the end?

Charles Richards / the Jericho Testing Laboratory / Anne Scott / Mrs Purvis / George Jackson / Edward Murdoch / Celia Richards

1 Please make an appointment with your own doctor if you wish to discuss the situation. Your local health clinic will be pleased to advise on diet and exercise over the next few months.

2 You must realize how difficult it would be for me if Celia found out about all this. It's over between us, and you will just have to accept that fact, however hard it seems at the moment.

3 You see, you're the only man I've ever really loved. You mean everything to me. And now – I just can't go on any more. But I don't want you to blame yourself – it's not your fault that things didn't work out. Remember me . . .

4 *Please* come and see me. I don't know who else to turn to. I never thought this would happen. I'm in desperate trouble, and I need help, and money. I just don't know what to do!

5 What would, or might, have happened if . . . ? Complete these sentences in your own words.

1 If Morse had become friendly with Anne after the party, . . .
2 Anne probably wouldn't have killed herself if . . .
3 If Jackson hadn't had a key to Anne's house, . . .
4 If Morse and Lewis had interviewed the Richards brothers together, . . .

113

ABOUT THE AUTHOR

Colin Dexter was born in 1930, in Stamford, Lincolnshire. He studied Latin and Ancient Greek at Cambridge University, and after graduating became a school-master, teaching Latin and Greek in schools in the Midlands. After that he worked as an educational administrator until his retirement in 1988.

Colin Dexter turned to crime writing when he was in his mid-40s, and has written thirteen detective novels so far, including *Last Bus to Woodstock* (1975), *Service of All the Dead* (1979), *The Wench is Dead* (1989), and *Death is Now My Neighbour* (1996). They are all based in and around the ancient university city of Oxford. Dexter (a former national champion in crossword competitions) says his novels fall into the 'whodunnit' category of crime writing, where complicated plots, 'with many a twist and many a turn', are designed to mystify the reader.

The novels are also famous for their two police detectives, Inspector Morse and his assistant, Sergeant Lewis. All the Morse stories have been adapted for television, attracting large audiences whenever they are shown. Public demand has been so great that further Morse stories have been specially written for television by other authors, and the series has been successfully exported to other countries.

The Dead of Jericho (1981) has the usual complicated plot, with twists and turns taking the reader off in many wrong directions. It also shows us Morse at his most human. He is a man who worries about losing his hair but is still interested in women, who enjoys a pint or two of beer while realizing it sometimes makes him forget things, and who listens to classical music in order to forget the loneliness of his life. It is his lack of confidence, his mistakes, his occasional bad temper, his meanness with money, and his very ordinariness that have made Morse such a popular fictional detective.

Dexter's novels have won several awards from the Crime Writers' Association: two have won Silver Daggers, another two have won Gold Daggers, and in 1997 Dexter was awarded the coveted Diamond Dagger for his services to crime literature. His books are among the best of 'puzzle' crime novels – not surprising, perhaps, from an author who takes delight in solving and setting some of the most difficult crosswords to appear in British newspapers.

ABOUT BOOKWORMS

OXFORD BOOKWORMS LIBRARY
Classics • True Stories • Fantasy & Horror • Human Interest
Crime & Mystery • Thriller & Adventure

The OXFORD BOOKWORMS LIBRARY offers a wide range of original and adapted stories, both classic and modern, which take learners from elementary to advanced level through six carefully graded language stages:

Stage 1 (400 headwords)	**Stage 4** (1400 headwords)
Stage 2 (700 headwords)	**Stage 5** (1800 headwords)
Stage 3 (1000 headwords)	**Stage 6** (2500 headwords)

More than fifty titles are also available on cassette, and there are many titles at Stages 1 to 4 which are specially recommended for younger learners. In addition to the introductions and activities in each Bookworm, resource material includes photocopiable test worksheets and Teacher's Handbooks, which contain advice on running a class library and using cassettes, and the answers for the activities in the books.

Several other series are linked to the OXFORD BOOKWORMS LIBRARY. They range from highly illustrated readers for young learners, to playscripts, non-fiction readers, and unsimplified texts for advanced learners.

Oxford Bookworms Starters   *Oxford Bookworms Factfiles*
Oxford Bookworms Playscripts   *Oxford Bookworms Collection*

Details of these series and a full list of all titles in the OXFORD BOOKWORMS LIBRARY can be found in the *Oxford English* catalogues. A selection of titles from the OXFORD BOOKWORMS LIBRARY can be found on the next pages.

Deadlock

SARA PARETSKY

Retold by Rowena Akinyemi

V. I. Warshawski, private investigator, Chicago, USA.

People imagine private detectives to be tired-looking men in raincoats, but Vic is female. She's tough, beautiful, carries a gun – and goes on asking questions until she gets answers.

When her cousin Boom Boom dies in an accident, Vic is naturally upset. She wants to know how and why the accident happened, and she isn't satisfied by the answers she gets. So she goes on asking questions . . . and more people start to die.

King's Ransom

ED McBAIN

Retold by Rosalie Kerr

'Calling all cars, calling all cars. Here's the story on the Smoke Rise kidnapping. The missing boy is eight years old, fair hair, wearing a red sweater. His name is Jeffry Reynolds, son of Charles Reynolds, chauffeur to Douglas King.'

The police at the 87th Precinct hate kidnappers. And these kidnappers are stupid, too. They took the wrong boy – the chauffeur's son instead of the son of the rich tycoon, Douglas King. And they want a ransom of $500,000.

A lot of money. But it's not too much to pay for a little boy's life . . . is it?

Brat Farrar

JOSEPHINE TEY

Retold by Ralph Mowat

'You look exactly like him! You can take the dead boy's place and no one will ever know the difference. You'll be rich for life!'

And so the plan was born. At first Brat Farrar fought against the idea; it was criminal, it was dangerous. But in the end he was persuaded, and a few weeks later Patrick Ashby came back from the dead and went home to inherit the family house and fortune. The Ashby family seemed happy to welcome Patrick home, but Brat soon realized that somewhere there was a time-bomb ticking away, waiting to explode . . .

This Rough Magic

MARY STEWART

Retold by Diane Mowat

The Greek island of Corfu lies like a jewel, green and gold, in the Ionian sea, where dolphins swim in the sparkling blue water. What better place for an out-of-work actress to relax for a few weeks?

But the island is full of danger and mysteries, and Lucy Waring's holiday is far from peaceful. She meets a rude young man, who seems to have something to hide. Then there is a death by drowning, and then another . . .

I, Robot

ISAAC ASIMOV

Retold by Rowena Akinyemi

A human being is a soft, weak creature. It needs constant supplies of air, water, and food; it has to spend a third of its life asleep, and it can't work if the temperature is too hot or too cold.

But a robot is made of strong metal. It uses electrical energy directly, never sleeps, and can work in any temperature. It is stronger, more efficient – and sometimes more human than human beings.

Isaac Asimov was one of the greatest science-fiction writers, and these short stories give us an unforgettable and terrifying vision of the future.

American Crime Stories

RETOLD BY JOHN ESCOTT

'Curtis Colt didn't kill that liquor store woman, and that's a fact. It's not right that he should have to ride the lightning – that's what prisoners call dying in the electric chair. Curtis doesn't belong in it, and I can prove it.' But can Curtis's girlfriend prove it? Murder has undoubtedly been done, and if Curtis doesn't ride the lightning for it, then who will?

These seven short stories, by well-known writers such as Dashiel Hammett, Patricia Highsmith, and Nancy Pickard, will keep you on the edge of your seat.